THE LEGEND OF DUTCHMAN'S MINE

Sheriff Thomas of Fenton's Creek is puzzled when an elderly recluse is murdered. This first killing is followed swiftly by another, leaving the small town at the centre of an affair which has even the government in Washington alarmed. Oblivious to the maelstrom of violence, young Harriet Thorndike arrives from Boston to attend her uncle's funeral. In no time at all, her own life is in jeopardy as she is caught in a desperate search for the treasure which is said to lie up in the Superstition Mountains of Arizona.

JETHRO KYLE

THE LEGEND OF DUTCHMAN'S MINE

Complete and Unabridged

LINFORD
Leicester

First published in Great Britain in 2017 by
Robert Hale
an imprint of The Crowood Press
Wiltshire

First Linford Edition
published 2020
by arrangement with
The Crowood Press
Wiltshire

A catalogue record for this book is available
from the British Library.

ISBN 978–1–4448–4369–9

Published by
F. A. Thorpe (Publishing)
Anstey, Leicestershire

Set by Words & Graphics Ltd.
Anstey, Leicestershire
Printed and bound in Great Britain by
T. J. International Ltd., Padstow, Cornwall

This book is printed on acid-free paper

Prologue

Superstition Mountain, Arizona 1848

Gabriel Thorndike calculated that they must have travelled fifteen miles or so from his home. Mind, it is hard to gauge such things accurately when you are blindfolded and travelling across rough and unfamiliar terrain. The Apaches had brought one of their own hardy little ponies for him to ride and all Thorndike needed to do was stay on the back of the creature until they reached their destination.

There was a lot of turning and doubling back on their tracks. Whether this was meant to disorient him and prevent him from finding his way to the place later, Thorndike could not say. It might equally well be the case that the party was moving through gullies and canyons, threading a circuitous route to their destination. Thorndike had a suspicion that they had been travelling upwards for a while, which led him in turn to suppose that perhaps they were now somewhere up on Superstition Mountain. At last, they stopped.

The man whose life he had saved undid his blindfold and Thorndike found the afternoon sun dazzling after having had his eyes closed for such a length of time. It took a while for him to be able to figure out what he was seeing. As he had suspected, they had travelled up into the Superstitions, but he had no idea which part of the range he had been taken to. All around was a rugged, dusty landscape, consisting mostly of bare rock. In front of Thorndike lay a shallow depression which looked like some sort of natural amphitheatre.

'Come,' said the man who had freed him of his blindfold. He was led down the slope into the centre of the arena-like space,

'In the time of our father's fathers,' said the Apache, 'this place was sacred both to the thunder god and also to Tobadzistsini, our god of war. It was they who filled the land here with sun's blood.'

'Sun's blood?' said Thorndike, 'I don't rightly understand you.'

The Apache went over to a heap of rocks and then came back with something hidden in his hand. He held it out to Thorndike. As he opened his fingers, there was a flash of yellow light. The Indian was holding a nugget of gold the size of a large pebble. He handed it to Thorndike, who thought that it must have weighed at least half a pound.

'So this is what you fellows call 'sun's blood',' said Thorndike. 'Is there much of it to be found here?'

'Look,' said the Apache. 'Look and see.' He stooped down and picked up a handful of the dry dust and broken chips of rock which littered the ground. He said again, 'Look!'

At first, Thorndike did not understand. Then he looked closer and suddenly realized that the handful of dirt contained flakes of native gold, along with larger chunks. It dawned on him that the entire, saucer-shaped depression in which he was standing, an area covering perhaps two or three acres, was quite literally covered with gold. The thought made him feel giddy. He turned to his guide and asked, 'Why have you brought me here?'

1

The house had been comprehensively ransacked, of that there could be no doubt. Sheriff Thomas looked around the room that had been the old man's study. The last time he had been here, maybe six months ago, the walls had been lined with books. Now, they had all been taken from the shelves and systematically mutilated. The spine of every volume had been slit open and the pages torn free. As each book had been treated in this way, so it was discarded in a corner. There must have been a three-foot-high pile of ripped-up books.

'What do you make to this?' asked Thomas' deputy.

'Damned if I know. They weren't looking for money, that much I do know.'

On the desk lay the dead man's gold

repeating pocket watch. It would have fetched at least $100 and yet whoever had searched the room had left it there as though it were not worth bothering about. Its former owner was sitting nearby, tied efficiently to a heavy oak chair. The old man had been stripped to the waist and there had been some preliminary attempts at torture. He had cheated his tormentors, though, by dying of what looked to the sheriff to be some species of seizure or stroke.

Deputy Bill Carter saw where his boss was looking and said, 'You think he told them what they wanted to know before he died?'

'Lord knows,' said Thomas. 'We would be better able to answer that question were we to have the faintest idea what it was they wished to find out.'

The rest of the large house had been searched as scientifically as the study. Every drawer had been removed, every cupboard rifled, every last scrap of paper seemingly scrutinized. Whoever had done this had had two and a half days to turn the place over. There were no live-in servants, just a woman who came to cook and clean during the week. She had a key of her own and had left her employer on the Friday evening and returned on Monday to find him dead.

'I suppose that his help, Mrs O'Grady is it, she has no idea what could be at the bottom of this?' asked Sheriff Thomas.

'Don't think so,' said Carter. 'She seems shocked rigid by the business. Says that the fellow was a perfect gentleman and had no interests in life beyond his books and writing.'

'Yes, I mind he wrote a couple of books. Are they anything to the purpose?'

'Wouldn't say so, boss. Indian legends, folklore and such.'

'Do we know if he had any family?' asked the sheriff. 'I seem to recollect a niece visiting every so often. Mark you, that would be some years since.'

'We'd best see his lawyer, maybe. Perhaps he had a will.'

★ ★ ★

Jacob Wexford, Attorney at Law, was sitting in his private office when one of the clerks knocked softly on the door. He bade the fellow enter and asked what was what.

'The sheriff is here, sir, and begs the favour of a few words.'

'Show him in, Timpkins, show him in.'

'Sheriff Thomas,' said Wexford, as his visitor entered the room, 'it is good to see you. Will you take a glass of sherry?'

'Not at such an early hour, begging your pardon, sir. But thank you for the offer.'

'To what do I owe this pleasure?'

'You act for Gabriel Thorndike, I think?' asked the sheriff.

'That is so.' Wexford did not enquire as to where the sheriff's questions were tending, having many years before discovered that the quieter you keep, the more you are apt to hear.

'I am sorry to have to tell you, sir, that Mr Thorndike is dead.'

'May I ask why the death of an old man should involve the sheriff's office?'

It struck Thomas that this was a time for plain speaking. He found dealing with old Mr Wexford irritating, due in large part to the attorney's affectation of talking like a character from one of Charles Dickens' novels, and wished only to extract whatever information the man might have. 'Thorndike was murdered some time since Friday. He had been subjected to torture before his death, cigarettes stubbed out on his body and suchlike. I am wondering if you know anything that might shed any light upon this crime?'

'Nothing at all, Sheriff', said Wexford. 'I drew up Mr Thorndike's will and also conducted some other business for him. That is all.'

'Who inherits his house and so on?'

'That's no secret. He has a niece in

Boston called Harriet. She used to stay with Mr Thorndike a good deal when she was a little girl. They were close.'

'How old would she be now?' asked Thomas.

'Twenty-two or thereabouts. I will notify her of her uncle's death. Unless, that is, she is suspected of his murder?'

Sheriff Thomas looked hard at Wexford, wondering if that was what passed for a joke with the old fox, but Wexford returned his gaze innocently. 'No,' said the sheriff, 'she is not suspected of murder.'

★   ★   ★

Sheriff Thomas and the lawyer were not the only people in town that morning who were talking over Gabriel Thorndike's death. In a dingy room over the Custom House Saloon, two other men were also discussing the case.

'That is the biggest waste of a Saturday and Sunday that I ever recall,' said one of the men.

'You talk like a woman,' said his companion, who was stripping down a pistol in order to oil and clean it. 'Waste of a Sunday! What would you otherwise have been doing yesterday, attending church or teaching in the Sunday School?'

'Do not push that line too far, Gonsalez,' said the first of the men to speak, 'it will not answer with me. You told me that Thorndike was as rich as Croesus. I saw no sign of it. From all the profit of these last few days, I might as well have taken that watch of his and be done with it.'

'You have not the patient mind, my friend,' said Gonsalez, a lean, dark man in his mid-thirties. 'Had you taken that watch, it would be proof that you had been in the house. It would tie you to the murder. You think such an uncommon article could be disposed of without question? It would have hanged you, that gold trinket. Besides, it is nothing, that watch. Listen now, I know

11

that the old man lived by selling gold. Not bullion, mark you, nor coins, but nuggets from river or mine. Did he look to you like one who made his living swinging a pickaxe in a mine?'

The other man, whose name was Dexter, laughed. 'No, I could not say that he did. What do you suggest we do now?'

'We wait. We wait and see what happens next. Somewhere in that house is the secret we are looking for. If we hurry, then the whole enterprise may miscarry.'

' 'The enterprise may miscarry'! You have a fancy way of talking, Gonsalez. I need not remind you that already this is a hanging matter. You think we should sit tight and wait for the law to catch a hold of us, so that we end up dangling on the end of a rope?'

Gonsalez regarded the other man steadily for a spell, long enough to make the other feel uncomfortable. Then he said, 'I hope that I am not wrong about you, Dexter. When first we met a few days ago, you represented yourself to me as a man who will stick at nothing. Yet what do I find? Only two days into the game and you are already whining about the fear of being hanged. Perhaps you are not the man I wanted for a business such as this.'

'I am game for anything, Gonsalez. I see no need to hazard my neck for nothing, though. If this partnership is to work, you had best open up a little and tell me more of what you purpose.'

Leon Gonsalez thought about this for a second, before saying, 'You are right, my friend. It is time for me to lie down, as a card player would say, and show you my hand.'

* * *

Harriet Thorndike was one of those alarming young females who just about that time were beginning to be called 'New Women'. Not that she was the sort who wore bloomers or smoked cigarettes in public. In Harriet

Thorndike's case, her feminism did not extend much further than refusing to abide by what she saw as outdated conventions and not allowing men to treat her like a prostitute or a doormat. When she received a wire telling her of the death of her Uncle Gabriel, she booked a ticket west that very day, regardless of what her mother represented to her as the impropriety of a young woman travelling alone by railroad. As she told her mother sharply, 'This is eighteen *eighty* six, not eighteen *fifty* six.'

On the first leg of her journey, south to New York, Harriet Thorndike did her best to figure out what her uncle's lawyer had meant when he told her that she must take great care, if she came west. Care about *what* precisely? She supposed that she would learn this when once she reached Fenton's Creek and took possession of the house that her uncle had bequeathed to her.

★ ★ ★

Leon Gonsalez had teamed up with his latest partner under singular and wholly unlooked-for circumstances. He had been heading for Fenton's Creek in order to question old Gabriel Thorndike in his own, inimitable fashion, when he had the misfortune to become embroiled with the faro table at a town some fifty miles east of his destination. One thing led to another and before he knew what had happened, Gonsalez had lost literally every cent he possessed. He did not even have enough money by the end of the night for a drink or to pay for a room somewhere. Gambling had almost been the ruin of him in the past and he was furiously angry with the man running the faro table for putting him into this embarrassing position.

After a chilly night spent walking up and down the deserted streets, Gonsalez was rewarded at about nine that morning by the sight of the fellow who had rooked him, riding off out of town. In the past, Leon Gonsalez had undertaken a little road-agent work when things were becoming awkward and he saw no reason not to do the same again now. Besides, he owed the dealer at the faro table an injury anywise for making him lose all his money.

Fortunately for both of them, the owner of the livery stable had demanded payment in advance for his horse's lodging for the night and so there was nothing to hinder Gonsalez from collecting his horse and riding out in pursuit of the man who had, as he saw it, robbed him of his money. He kept a discreet distance behind the fellow, waiting until they had left behind the patchwork quilt of fields which surrounded the town. The waylaying of lone travellers in this manner was a good deal less common than it had been twenty years earlier, in the aftermath of the War Between the States. Justice was a sight quicker to catch up with men carrying out such activities too, and Gonsalez had no wish to find himself crossing swords with the law. He was wanted for various crimes in several states and, worse still, he had been sentenced to death in Mexico just after the fall of the Emperor, although he had managed to elude the firing squad. Some of those whom he had offended in those days had long and vengeful memories and he had no desire to be pushed back across the border by the Americans.

When Gonsalez judged that they were far enough from town, he spurred on his horse and made to catch up with his quarry. They were in an area of dusty, rocky hills, which rose on either side of the road, occasionally blocking the view of the road ahead. This was the case now and he had lost sight of the rider ahead of him. It was no matter though, because there was no other track and nowhere for the man to go except onwards along the road. He cantered around a fall of rocks and stumbled upon a wholly unexpected sight.

The man he intended to rob had halted and was being threatened by a younger man with a handkerchief tied round the lower half of his face in approved bandit style. It was plain to Gonsalez that this man was in the very process of robbing the fellow who was his own legitimate victim. He rode forward and drew his pistol.

It was a delicate situation; not least for the faro dealer who, although he had in the past been robbed, had never yet had the novel experience of thieves lining up to deprive him of his money. The man who had stopped him on the road was now facing off with a swarthy and good-looking newcomer whom he recognized from the previous night. Both men had guns in their hands and neither seemed disposed to back down.

'What's to do?' asked the young man with his face half covered. 'Are you the law?'

'I, the law?' said Gonsalez, his white teeth flashing for a moment in amusement. 'No, nothing of the sort. I am about to take this man's money.'

'That won't do,' said the other man gruffly, 'I am robbing him. You had best find another mark.'

'I am not such a one as allows others to dictate to him his actions,' said Gonsalez, still in an amiable tone of voice. 'You had best leave while you are still able.'

'Oh, so that's the game, is it? I tell you now, I ain't about to go anywhere. You would do better to stick your head in a hornets' nest than muscle in on my business. Be off with you.'

The faro dealer coughed softly to attract their attention, before saying, 'Gentlemen, could you hurry up and decide which of you will be stealing my money? I have an appointment.'

Gonsalez turned to the man and asked casually, 'I dare say that you recognize me, do you not, my friend?'

'Why yes, you are that fellow who lost so much at my table last night. I recollect that your name is Gonsalez.'

Acknowledging that he knew Gonsalez' face and name in this way was a terrible mistake; the last that ever the faro dealer would make in the whole course of his life. Without moving his position or giving the least indication of his intention, the Mexican twisted his hand a little and shot the man, his bullet hitting the faro dealer in the chest. Looking enormously surprised at this turn of events, the man said, 'My God, you have shot me, sir!' Then he slumped sideways and fell from the horse, one ankle remaining entangled in the stirrup. The horse, already spooked by the shot, now took off as fast as it was able with a dead man hanging on one side.

Gonsalez burst suddenly into laughter. 'After him,' he cried, 'or we shall neither of us have any profit from his death.' The two of them galloped off after the fleeing horse, Gonsalez laughing in delight until even the other man smiled reluctantly at the ridiculous situation they now found themselves in.

When once they had caught up with the horse and freed it of its former owner, Gonsalez and the other man stood over the corpse, facing each other once again. Having joined together in pursuit, though, there was less tension in the air and the chances of a sudden shootout seemed to be greatly lessened.

'What say you to share and share alike?' suggested Gonsalez in a friendly way. 'We have both joined in the hunt and so we both deserve to share in the spoils.'

The other man was still a little dubious about the Mexican. Having seen how readily the other had shot down an unarmed man just a few minutes earlier, he felt that this was a man who would bear a little watching and upon whom a prudent man might be best advised not to turn his back. At length, he said, 'All right, but you search the body and see what you come up with.'

Gonsalez laughed. 'What, you are squeamish about a dead man?'

'No, I ain't squeamish. I just don't trust you not to shoot me in the back while I am bending over him.'

At this, Gonsalez laughed uproariously and clapped the other man on the back, saying, 'I think that you and I are going to be friends.'

So it was that something over a week later, Leon Gonsalez and Alfred Dexter were sitting in the cramped little room above the Custom House, while the Mexican told his companion what he knew about Gabriel Thorndike. He had enlisted Dexter's help in searching the Thorndike house, without revealing any more than the bare fact that the fellow had some sort of treasure map which would lead them to untold riches. Gonsalez had not gone into details. Now, he did so.

'Tell me, my friend,' said Gonsalez, 'did you ever hear the tale of the Lost Dutchman's Mine?'

'I heard it. Never reckoned much to it, though. I heard of other wonderful places too, where a man could just pick up all the gold he liked from the ground. Never heard of anybody who found such a place, though, and that's a fact. It's like that Sugar Cane Mountain Land that you hear the coloured boys sing about. A story for children.'

'The Dutchman's Mine is different. It exists. I told you that we needed to find out from the old man where his money came from? I did not tell you, though, that I already knew the answer to that question. I was hoping that he would give us directions, but the bastard died. It was a thousand pities.'

'Strikes me, Gonsalez, as you have been holding back on a mite more information than I rightly care for. I don't mind being mixed up in murder, but I want to know what it is for. You would do well to remember this another time. I will not be your fall guy.'

The Mexican smiled easily. He said, 'What's done is written. There is no use, as you Americans would say, in crying over the milk, when once it is spilled. Is that not so?' He went on, 'None of this is to the purpose. When he was a young man, Thorndike lived in

Arizona, not far from Superstition Mountain. It is Apache country and the mountain, which is really a group of mountains, is sacred to their heathen gods. They visit death upon intruders. At the heart of the mountains is a small valley where there is abundant gold. In 1820 or thereabouts, a German called Jacob Waltz found this place while prospecting.'

'German?' said Dexter, 'I thought it was supposed to be the Dutchman's Mine? Or was there another fellow later who was Dutch?'

Leon Gonsalez fancied himself as something of a raconteur and did not like to be interrupted in this way. He said irritably, 'No, it was the same man. He told people that he was 'Deutsch', that is German in his own language. Some muddled this word up with 'Dutch'. Anyway, Waltz found this location where gold was just lying on the ground. It was the richest reef of gold that anybody had ever seen. The wind and sand had worn away the gold-bearing rock and left nuggets of gold everywhere.'

'I have done some prospecting on my own account,' said Dexter, 'and it is usually water which wears away the rock. You say that here it was the wind? That may be so.'

'It *is* so, not *may* be so. Waltz drew a map of the place and went back a number of times. Then he died and the map came into the possession of others. During the war, two soldiers found the hidden valley and came away with much gold. Others were not so lucky and were killed by the Apaches for profaning their holy ground.'

'It is an interesting story, Gonsalez,' said Dexter, 'but you have not told me where the old man we killed fits into the scheme of things.'

'Your impatience is a failing, my friend,' said the Mexican, with a flash of ill humour. 'If you do not curb it, who knows what evil it might bring upon you?'

'I don't need no lessons from you,'

said the other, 'nor threats neither, if that is what this talk of evil is tending towards. I am not a man to be bluffed by such words and you would do well to remember it.'

'Cha!' said Gonsalez, 'We digress. We must not fall out or, as you have told me before, we might both hang. Thorndike had many years ago a little house nigh to Superstition Mountain. Do not ask how I know this, but only be assured that it is so. I do not know the details of what chanced, but he did a good turn to an Apache shaman or what you might call a medicine man. As a consequence, he was allowed to visit the site of the gold. I have reason to think that he went back over the years and that he knew how to get there.'

'So you are telling me that this is a busted flush? The old man knew the secret of some great fortune, but that he died without telling us?'

'Do you think that it would be in reason for Thorndike never to write down the location of the mine? I told you when we searched his house that we were to look for any map or set of instructions for a journey. I did not tell you why and now I have done so. Somewhere in that house is the answer to our quest. It is hidden, that is all. We sit tight now and wait for somebody else to find the clue. Then, Tcheee . . . ' Gonsalez made a gesture which suggested a throat being cut.

'You are sure about all this?' asked Dexter. 'This is not some mad snipe hunt?'

'Snipe hunt, snipe hunt! What ails you man? I have offered you the greatest chance of your wretched life and you talk to me of snipe hunts.'

Alfred Dexter gazed impassively at the Mexican. 'I will go along with you for now, Gonsalez,' he said, 'but I hope that this is a true bill. What do you suggest we do now?'

'I told you. We wait. Somebody will come to the house soon and then we shall see what we shall see. I believe that whoever takes possession of the place might know better than we where the old man hid anything of value to us in this search. And then!' Gonsalez stretched out his hand and made a grabbing movement, to indicate that he would be able to snatch away this precious information from whoever unearthed it in the dead man's house.

2

As soon as Harriet Thorndike arrived in Fenton's Creek, she wired her mother to let her know that she was safe and then made her way to Jacob Wexford's office. The office did not look noticeably different from how she remembered it when she came there with her uncle as a little girl.

A clerk ushered her through to Wexford's inner sanctum and he rose to greet her. 'Harriet, or I suppose that I should call you Miss Thorndike, now that you are grown up.'

'Harriet will do just fine, sir. Your wire did not make it clear how my uncle died. Was he ill for a long time? I am surprised that he did not write and tell me; I would willingly have come to nurse him.'

'Your Uncle Gabriel was not ill for a single day that I ever heard tell of. He was murdered.'

'Murdered? Who would want to kill an old dear like Uncle Gabriel?'

The lawyer said nothing for a space, staring at her in a disconcerting way. At last he asked, 'What are your plans? Those touching upon your late uncle's house, I mean. You know that you are his sole heir?'

'Yes, he told me. You have not said how he was murdered or why.'

'As to that, I could not say. Somebody entered his house, tied him to a chair and tormented him. He died as a result, which is why the sheriff is treating it as murder.'

Harriet shuddered. 'What a terrible thing. Did he suffer?'

'I wouldn't know,' said the old attorney, 'you had best ask the sheriff. Might I be permitted to give you some advice? As an old friend of your uncle's, that is to say?'

'Of course, Mr Wexford,' said Harriet, wondering what could be coming next.

'Well then, I would leave Fenton's

Creek this very day and leave me to sell the house and send on old Mr Thorndike's belongings to you in Boston.'

'Oh, but I couldn't do that,' said Harriet in surprise, 'I have only just got here. I shall be staying in the house for a week or so and going through Uncle Gabriel's effects.'

'The house was searched and many things destroyed. It would not be a nice place to stay. Why not leave the task to my firm?'

'Do you think that I might come to harm if I stay there?' the girl asked bluntly.

'The thought had crossed my mind,' admitted the lawyer.

* * *

Sheriff Thomas was not a happy man. Murders were rare in Fenton's Creek and when once they had been committed, it was never hard to find the killer. In the last eight years, there had been six such crimes. In five cases, the murderer was the husband or wife of the victim and in the sixth case it was a wandering cowboy who got drunk and began firing off his pistol at random one night. The sheriff could not recall hearing of any unsolved murder in the town, even before he himself became sheriff.

What was so troubling about the death of Gabriel Thorndike was that there seemed to be neither rhyme nor reason behind it. The motive was clearly not theft and nobody could have had a personal grudge against such a good-natured and benevolent old fellow as Thorndike. It was a regular conundrum. While he was sitting with his feet up on the desk in his office, musing along these lines, the door to the street opened and in walked a young woman.

The woman who entered his office was young, so young that she was really little more than a girl, for all that she had her hair up and was dressed so stylishly. Thomas guessed her age at eighteen or nineteen.

'Sheriff Thomas?' she asked, and her voice acted like a tonic upon the jaded lawman. She was so bright and enthusiastic; so full of life.

'That's me,' said the sheriff, taking his feet from the desk, feeling that it looked a little slovenly and discourteous in the presence of a lady. 'How may I help you?'

'I am enquiring about the death of my uncle. Gabriel Thorndike, that is. Mr Wexford, the lawyer, said that you could tell me about it.'

Sheriff Thomas felt a natural reluctance to discuss in detail such an unpleasant business, especially with a lady. He limited himself to saying, 'I think that your uncle disturbed some burglars, perhaps. They killed him.'

The girl frowned. 'That's funny. Mr Wexford said that he had been tied up and tormented. Why would burglars do such a thing?'

'I couldn't say, I'm sure. You need

not trouble about it, though, my investigations are in hand. Are you in town for long?'

'I shall be attending the funeral tomorrow and then sorting out my uncle's affairs.'

'Are you staying at a hotel or do you have friends hereabouts?'

'Hotel?' said the girl in surprise. 'No, I shall be living at my uncle's house.'

The sheriff looked up swiftly. 'I wouldn't do that, you know.'

'Why not?'

'In case those who killed your uncle should return.'

Harriet Thorndike said only, 'I shall be attending the funeral tomorrow and perhaps we shall meet there?'

Thomas rose and wished the girl good day. He was uneasy in his mind about the whole business and would be greatly relieved when that determined and energetic-looking young lady had left town again.

★   ★   ★

Harriet Thorndike was shocked and dismayed at the state of her uncle's house. His precious books had every one been torn up and cast in a heap. It all seemed so senseless. She wandered around the place, observing the apparently wanton damage caused to the property in every room in the house. Instinctively, she felt that those who had ransacked the place in this fashion must have been looking for something in particular. And she had a good idea where whatever it was they had been seeking was to be found!

All sorts of junk was stored in the cupboard under the stairs. Old pictures, enamelled pitchers, broken lamps and all those other bits and pieces that a thrifty old man like Gabriel Thorndike could never have brought himself to throw out for good. Harriet went into the kitchen and fetched a small oil lamp. She lit it and then investigated more thoroughly the space beneath the stairs. As a child, this had been her 'den' when she was staying with her uncle. At the back of the space were some vertical boards, which looked as though they blocked off the final part of the area beneath the stairs.

Wiggling one of the boards allowed Harriet to prise it loose and then she could remove the others. Revealed was a tiny room, no more than six feet long. This was her old secret place, where she had stored her treasures as a little girl and had also curled up to read books and write her diary. Her uncle had even allowed her to have a candle in there and how she had not burned the house down in consequence was something of a miracle. Amazingly, some of her old belongings were still here. Sketches that she had made, a bunch of dried grasses and interestingly shaped pebbles which she had collected from the river bank. There was something else as well; a large, leather-bound book which looked like the sort of ledger that might be found in a bank. Just as she had guessed, her uncle had taken over her little secret room when once she had grown up, and used it to store his own secrets. Harriet lifted up the book and took it into the kitchen. Laying the heavy volume on the table, she opened it at the first page and read:

NIAY OSETHAY LAY ASWAY VINGLIAY NIAY ACHEAPAY ERRITORYTAY; GHNIAY OTAY PERSTITIONSUAY OUNTAIN-MAY

Despite the grief that she was feeling for the loss of her beloved uncle, the young woman gave a sudden squeal of delight as she recognized what was written in the book. It was Pig Latin; an old code, one first used, at least according to her uncle, by Thomas Jefferson.

Calling Pig Latin a code is perhaps somewhat of a misnomer. It is formed by removing the first consonant or consonant cluster from the beginning of each word and placing it at the end, followed by the letters 'A' and 'Y'. The result looks a little like Latin. Harriet guessed correctly that her uncle had written like this not in order to frustrate a determined code breaker, but merely to prevent any casual reader from opening the book and seeing at once what he had set down there. She had once been perfectly fluent at this and it took her only a few seconds to translate the opening passage as:

In those days, I was living in the Apache territory; nigh to Superstition Mountain.

The girl brewed a pot of coffee and then settled down to read the book which her uncle had evidently been at such pains to keep from prying eyes.

In those days, I was living in the Apache territory; nigh to Superstition Mountain. I say Apache, but the Indians there were really Chiricahua. Technically, they belong to the Apache, but in reality they are very different.

I was collecting ethnological data on the tribe; legends, folklore and much else besides. To do this, I lived in an abandoned farmhouse within view of the sacred mountain. Late one night, I was writing up my notes by candlelight, when I became aware of a furtive scratching noise outside. Of course, I was used to various wild animals prowling about, but this sounded to my ear different. There was a purposeful air to the noise.

I felt a little uneasy, rational man though I am. I recalled legends of the wendigo and other cannibal spirits said to haunt the northern wilderness. Could this be a Mexican version of such a malevolent ghost? At length, I lost patience with myself and, picking up my rifle and cocking it, I threw open the door, crying, 'Stand to, 'less you want a ball through your heart!'

On the very doorstep lay a grievously injured man; an Indian. He was no older than me, say about twenty-five or so. He had been shot through the shoulder and looked to me to be as weak as a kitten. He had lost a lot of blood and had obviously seen the light from my candle and made for the old house. By the by, I call it a 'house' but truth to tell, it was little better than a one-room hut.

'God save us,' I said, 'let's get you inside.' The fellow could barely raise his head; he must have used all his energy simply in getting to my hut. I hauled him inside and somehow man-handled him onto the bed. He lay there, bleeding like a stuck hog. I did my best to bind up his wound and stop the bleeding, but I very much expected him to die during the night. Besides the bed, I had a table and chair at which I wrote. I dozed a little, with my head resting on my arms as I leaned on the table and then, before I knew it, it was dawn. I went to tend to my guest and found to my surprise that not only was he not dead, but that he seemed to have recovered somewhat.

'Will you have something to eat and

drink?' I asked him in his own language. He stared at me in astonishment to hear me speaking the Chiricahua dialect, but he indicated his assent. I gave him some cold porridge and a cup of water. He watched me suspiciously all the while.

After he had eaten and drunk, he said, 'Of you, I have heard. You are the white-eye who listens to mysteries and makes a record of them. Some of our young men say that you should be killed. Others say that you are a good man.'

The Chiricahua call white men the 'white-eyes'. I hardly knew what to say to that and so I remained silent. After a space, the man on the bed spoke again. He said, 'More white-eyes are coming all the time. Soon, they will drive the Chiricahua from their land. I have seen this in a dream.'

I am ashamed to say that I was a young man in those days and I merely smiled at the man's fears. It seemed so unlikely to me; there was plenty of room for everybody in the land. How

41

could it be possible that the Indians would be made to leave their own land? Remember, this was thirty or forty years ago. I said to the fellow, 'No, the white-eyes only wish to live in peace and farm the land here. There is surely room for both peoples?'

God help me, for I actually believed this then. As I say, remember that I was little more than a boy in those days and a lot has changed since then.

'Every day, more and more white-eyes come from the east. They do not want the Chiricahua to stay,' continued my guest. 'One day, there will be nowhere at all for our people to live.'

At the time, this all seemed quite mad and I simply couldn't see any sense in what the fellow was saying. Of course, we all know now that he was perfectly correct.

Goyahkla, for that was his name, stayed with me for a week. When he left, he told me that I had saved his life and that he would repay me. I brushed aside his gratitude, but I suppose that he was right; I had saved his life.

I spent my days travelling about the country near to my little house and after speaking to Goyahkla, I began to see that there might be something in what he was saying. There were white gold prospectors, settlers, hunters and soldiers and it was becoming harder and harder for me to track down Indians who would trust me and be ready to share their stories with me. I have to say that I did not take overmuch to the attitude of many of the white people I met towards the Indians. They talked of them as though they were rats or cockroaches who had to be exterminated.

A few weeks after I had bade farewell to Goyahkla and almost forgotten about him, he returned one morning, just as I was sitting outside with my breakfast. He was accompanied by two other men; grim-looking warriors. He told me that he had come to repay me for my help. I told him that it was not necessary, but I could see that he would be hugely offended if I refused. In the end, I agreed to go off with him and the two men who were with him. They had brought a spare mount for me. I had a horse of my own of course, but the sturdy ponies that the Chiricahua rode were better for rough terrains.

Goyahkla apologised, but told me that he would have to bind my eyes, as we were going to a secret place of the Apache people. The journey took most of the day and when we arrived, I found myself in a small valley in the middle of the mountains. Some freak geological process had exposed a rich vein of native gold to the surface and the wind and sand had worn away the surrounding rock. There was more gold in that place than anybody can conceive. It lay around like discarded trash. The Chiricahua called gold 'Sun's blood' and it was somehow sacred to them. Goyahkla, though, was a shaman and could override their taboos. He told me that I could take as much of the stuff as I could carry away.

When we got back to my house, I told Goyahkla that I had been observing the situation, in the light of what he had said, and thinking of his vision of the future. I confessed to him that he was right and pledged myself to help him, if I was able, to hold on to what his people had had for many hundreds of years; their very land. So began the strangest friendship that I ever could have imagined.

Harriet stopped reading her uncle's book and stood up. She went over to the window and looked out onto the neat little garden that surrounded the house. She hardly knew what to do next, because she had not the slightest doubt that this book and the information which it probably contained was what the men who killed her uncle had been seeking. The question was, what was she going to do about it?

★　★　★

Despite the anger aroused by the nature of his death, the funeral of Gabriel Thorndike was a surprisingly good-humoured affair. Everybody had some pleasant memory of the old man and those whom his niece invited back to the house afterwards were soon exchanging their stories about the old man's eccentric, but lovable, ways.

'Do you recall when he visited the orphans' asylum over in Snowflake?' asked the priest who had officiated. 'Swore the superintendent to secrecy and then left enough money to buy every child a toy. It was too good a story for the folk at the orphanage to keep to themselves. When it became known here in Fenton's Creek, the old fellow couldn't walk down the street without some woman stopping him and telling him that he was a regular Santa Claus.'

One of the listeners laughed at the memory. 'Yes, Gabriel, he was morti-fied. You know how he hated fuss. He hid in here for a week, you know, after that story went the rounds and only set foot out of the house after dark. He was that horrified at being told what a good man he was.'

Another man said, 'I don't believe there was a beggar for a hundred miles in any direction that did not sooner or later fetch up here with some hard luck story. Old Thorndike would be studying away or writing about Indian legends or some such and used to get wild if he was disturbed. Not one of those men ever left empty-handed, though. I never knew the like.'

Harriet Thorndike felt the tears pricking the back of her eyes and rushed from the room just as the rainbow flashes told her that she would any moment be bursting into tears. This was a public humiliation that she was determined to avoid. After retreating upstairs, wiping her eyes and blowing her nose, she thought over all that she had heard. That her uncle had been generous and kind, she had known from her earliest years. That he had been very rich, she was only now realizing. And after reading the opening pages of his secret book the previous day, she now had a shrewd notion as to the origin of his wealth. She glanced from the window and saw two men passing the house. They looked vaguely familiar, as though she had seen them before. Had they been at the funeral?

* * *

Leon Gonsalez and Alfred Dexter strolled past the Thorndike place with an air of affected nonchalance. They had been in the burying ground earlier that day, although had not attended the funeral itself. Instead, they took a bunch of flowers with them and arranged these artistically on the grave of a man whom neither of them had known in life. While engaged in this pretty little piece of play-acting, they managed to gain a glimpse at the mourners around Gabriel Thorndike's open grave. It was common knowledge that old Thorndike's niece had come to town to sort out the old man's affairs and the funeral was a good opportunity for the two men to sneak a look at her. Gonsalez in particular was pleased with what he saw.

After Dexter and Gonsalez had left the graveyard, the latter said to his companion, 'Young, you mark; very young. And trusting too, I should not be surprised to learn. You see now, my friend, the rewards which patience bring to us, no?'

The practical Dexter said, 'I know you have an eye for the ladies, Gonsalez, but I don't figure none that this helps us in the present case.'

'Do you not?' said the other. 'But you are, as they say, one step behind me.'

'I might have remarked before, Gonsalez, that all this riddling talk irks me, I am a man who likes matters to be spoken of plainly.'

'Well then, to speak plainly I think that I might be able to charm this innocent young maiden into letting me in on whatever secrets she has uncovered there. You have heard, they say that she stayed much with the old man when she was a child. Hear what I say, she will by now know something of that which we seek.'

After everybody had gone home, and left her by herself, Harriet fetched her uncle's book from its hiding place, with a view to continuing her reading of his story. As she brought it into the kitchen, something fluttered to the floor. It was a small sheet of paper covered in Pig Latin and also bearing a sketch map. With mounting excitement, the young woman smoothed the paper out on the table and set to translating it into plain English. Unless she missed her guess, this was a set of instructions for reaching the location where her uncle had seen all that gold.

Some of the instructions, when once she had decoded them, seemed straightforward enough; 'Head for the needle of rock', for instance. But of others, she could make not the slightest sense. What on earth could he have meant by, 'Travel half a mile cat' or 'Turn fish and keep moving until you reach a narrow gully'?

* * *

Harriet Thorndike never knew how close she had come that evening to meeting the same fate as her late uncle. Gonsalez was happy, as he had intimated to Dexter, to try and seduce the girl; but he was equally ready to tie her up and torture her to death if that would better serve his ends. In the event, he did not have the chance to attempt either course of action, because before the sun went down that day, he was on the run for murder. This is what happened.

The Mexican was getting tired of being cooped up in that little room over the saloon. Dexter was not much company for a gregarious fellow like Gonsalez and so he had decided that before he paid a visit to the old man's niece later that night, he would find some amusement. He accordingly left Dexter to his own devices and went off in search of entertainment. Both he and Dexter were pretty flush, because the late faro dealer had had plenty of cash money on his person when Gonsalez shot him.

There were four saloons in Fenton's Creek and one, the Silver Spur, was renowned for the high-stakes poker games that were played there. After robbing the faro dealer, Gonsalez had a few dollars in his pocket and felt as though his luck was running in the right direction. It was just the time to find a game of cards. He found four men playing a lively game in the Silver Spur and they were only too pleased to allow the Mexican to join them at their table. What Gonsalez did not know is that these men were a travelling group who, while posing as casual acquaintances who had only just met, were in fact working their way to California by running rigged poker games.

It has to be said that the four of them were exceedingly good at what they did and even Gonsalez, who was the most untrusting of men, suspected nothing until he found his ace-high full house, upon which he had bet all the money he had, topped by four sevens. At this point, he tried to talk the men round to his position as reasonably as he knew how.

'I know what you boys are about,' said Gonsalez pleasantly, 'I had a seven when I threw down in the last hand. It cannot have come round again so soon. You are cheats. Just return my money and we will go no further down this sorrowful road.' The others laughed, which infuriated the Mexican. 'I will ask once more,' he said, 'and then you must bide the consequences.'

'Get out of here, you greaseball!' said the man who had dealt him the full house. 'We do not like sore losers.' The words were scarcely out of his mouth when Gonsalez, who took it particularly ill when folk twitted him about his

Hispanic origins by using terms such as 'greaseball', had grabbed the man by his shirt-front and hauled him to his feet. He then twisted the fellow round so that he was facing the table and acting as a shield; just on the off-chance that any of his friends should feel inclined towards any gunplay.

At the same moment that Gonsalez had yanked the crooked dealer to his feet, he somehow contrived to produce from within his boot a razor-sharp stiletto, which he pressed against the throat of the man he was now using as a hostage. It made no difference though, because these fellows were obviously not so fond of each other that they would scruple to hazard the lives of the others. The man opposite suddenly had in his hand a tiny muff pistol, something in the Derringer line. When once he caught sight of this, the Mexican did not hesitate. He drew the thin blade with great force across the throat of the man behind whom he was sheltering. As the arterial blood began to spray, like the contents of a shaken soda siphon, into the faces of the other three card players, he pushed the dying man into them. The table went over, there was a crack from the Derringer and in the ensuing chaos, with other customers of the saloon diving for cover at the sound of gunfire, Leon Gonsalez made a swift exit from the place.

3

Harriet Thorndike had given up in exasperation on the supposed treasure map and returned to her uncle's book. She read the next entry with growing interest.

Goyahkla came back several times in the next month or two. He seemed fascinated about what I was doing and could not quite grasp why I was interested in his people's legends and myths. I explained that I wanted to record these for the future, because although now they were all passed down by word of mouth, some day, something might happen to prevent that. How right I was.

That autumn, Goyahkla came again to me and asked how much I cared to help the Chiricahua with their struggle for survival. I told him that I would do anything I could to help. He had already been of immense help to me in sending other members of the tribe to talk to me and allowing me to speak to women and children as well. With his blessing, I had more or less free access to their villages. Anyway, that day he said to me, 'Would you help the Chiricahua resist the white-eyes who are pushing them away from their land?'

'I would do that, yes.' I told him.

'The sun's blood from Sacred Mountain was given to my people by the gods. It is ours to do with as we will. The white-eyes would cheat us if we tried to sell it. Will you sell it, if we bring it to you?'

I did not ask what they wanted with money. Their cause was just and so I agreed to help. Goyahkla took me up into Superstition Mountain again and this time I was not blindfolded. I was allowed to roam about the area at will.

There were traces of some mining activity there; what looked to be pit-props, bleached by the sun. I guessed that some white men had stumbled on the place by chance and tried to exploit it; although why they would have been thinking of digging down, with so much gold just lying on the ground, was a mystery to me. Under my direction, the Chiricahua gathered up only the smallest of the nuggets. Some of those chunks of native gold were the size of my fist, but I did not want to give anybody cause to start asking questions. The last thing that we needed was some sort of gold rush in that part of the territory. Once white men began swarming in for gold, it would be all up with Goyahkla's people.

I suppose that even then, right at the beginning of the business, I knew deep inside that the Apache would be using the money which I obtained for them in order to purchase guns. This did not strike me then as any bad thing for them.

There was a sharp rapping at the front

door and Harriet pulled a face in irritation. She considered not answering the door, but then reflected that it was perhaps somebody who had known her uncle and wished to pass on condolences. It would be unforgivably rude to ignore such a call. She reluctantly rose and then, as an afterthought, put her uncle's book out of sight in one of the cupboards. Then she went to see who the visitor was.

At about the same time that Harriet Thorndike was answering the front door of her late uncle's house, there came a knock on the door of the room where Gonsalez and Dexter were staying. Dexter was alone in the room and had taken the precaution of locking the door after his new partner had gone off in search of amusement. He was lying on one of the cots reading a dime novel entitled *The Killer of Deadwood Gulch* and was so immersed in it that he did not hear the first knock. When he failed to open the door at once, there came a perfect fusillade of harder blows, as if the person without were in a great hurry.

'All right, all right,' grumbled Dexter, getting up from the bed. 'Hold your horses, I'm a-coming.' He unlocked the door and almost before the lock was sprung, Gonsalez was in the room. Even in the dim and uncertain light of the oil lamp, it was plain as a pikestaff to Alfred Dexter that his partner was in some sort of trouble. The man's eyes were glittering and he was breathing heavily. He gave the appearance not of fear, but of a man in a state of great excitement. 'Gonsalez, what troubles you, man?' said Dexter.

'Ah,' said the Mexican, 'I find I must leave this town for a spell. It is nothing, a mere bagatelle.'

'A what?' said Dexter. 'What are you about?'

'I am leaving for a while. You recall that little stone shelter that we passed on the way to this place? Not far from the roadside, about ten miles hence?'

'Yes, what of it?'

'I must lie low now. I will meet you at that place each night at ten, is that clear?'

Alfred Dexter was no great shakes in the brains department, but even he could see well enough that something was seriously amiss. He said, 'Gonsalez, unless you tell me what has happened, I will not be coming anywhere to see you.'

'Ach, very well. I killed a man tonight. That is all, and now I must stay out of the way for a while.'

'You killed a man?' asked Dexter, in amazement. 'Why?'

'He cheated me at cards.'

'Gonsalez, you mad bastard. You cannot kill a man for some such trifle. Is this what you meant when you talked to me of patience?'

Before Dexter knew what was what, the Mexican had him pinned against the wall, with a bloody knife pressed against the artery at the side of his neck, saying 'Do not get crosswise to me. I will kill you as readily as I did the other.'

'All right, don't take on. I will come and see you and bring some vittles too, if you like. You are a mighty touchy fellow, Gonsalez. Is the law onto this business yet?'

Gonsalez sheathed his knife. 'If they are not yet, then that time cannot be long delayed. I will see you by that shelter tomorrow night at ten. And set a watch upon the old man's house and see what is going on there. I do not purpose to let this little mishap spoil our game.' The Mexican gathered up his belongings and vanished into the night.

★ ★ ★

Standing on the doorstep of Gabriel Thorndike's house was a young man of about thirty years of age. He was smartly dressed and looked to Harriet as though his normal habitat was probably a big city back east, rather than a small town like Fenton's Creek. 'May I help you?' she asked.

'I am looking for Miss Harriet Thorndike,' said the man. 'According to Sheriff Thomas, she is to be found here. Have I the pleasure of addressing Miss Thorndike?'

His voice was cultured, urbane and definitely eastern. She would not be surprised to learn that he hailed, like her, from Boston. 'I am Miss Thorndike,' she said. 'What can I do for you?'

'It is somewhat delicate. Perhaps we could discuss it inside?'

The young woman was beginning to grow uneasy. She had already been warned about staying in this house alone and now here was a complete stranger, trying to talk his way into the house with her. She said, the lie coming to her as an inspiration, 'I'm sorry, but I already have a visitor here. My uncle's attorney and I are going over his affairs. Perhaps you could leave your card and I will get in touch with you?'

The man's lips twitched slightly at

the corners, as though he were restraining the impulse to smile. Instead he reached into an inside pocket and withdrew a silver card case. He extracted a visiting card and handed it to Harriet, saying gravely, 'I am staying at the Supreme. I would be pleased if you were to call on me tomorrow morning. It is a matter of some urgency.' He paused and then said, his eyes unmistakably twinkling now, 'By the by, you might pass on my congratulations to Mr Wexford. For a man of his advanced years, he surely is a most remarkable athlete. I left him at his office not fifteen minutes since and he has evidently sprinted through a circuitous route in order to arrive at this house before me. It is an uncommon feat. Goodnight, Miss Thorndike.'

Harriet felt herself blushing crimson like a schoolgirl. To be caught out in a lie like that! She wondered what business the fellow could have had with the sheriff and old Mr Wexford. The card gave his name as Patrick McFadden and an address in Washington DC.

★ ★ ★

By the time Sheriff Thomas arrived at the Silver Spur, the place was all but deserted. The only people on the premises were the barkeep, the three living men who had been playing poker with Gonsalez and their dead companion, who was lying dead upon the floor. It was possible that the three men might, like the other patrons of the Silver Spur, have slipped quietly off, if the barkeep had not fetched a sawn-off scatter gun from under the bar and kept them covered as soon as he heard shooting from their table and saw that somebody had been killed. His back had been turned at the crucial moment and he'd seen nothing of the altercation with Gonsalez. As a consequence, he naturally assumed that one of them had shot the man who was lying dead on the floor. Despite their angry protestations, he kept the three of them under guard, while somebody went for the sheriff. While he did so, all the other men in the room suddenly recollected urgent business that they had elsewhere and left, more or less *en masse*.

Sheriff Thomas was not overly keen on cardsharps and bunko artists. He had been aware that four men were running a game at the Silver Spur which had led to some acrimonious scenes after large sums of money had been lost. Still and all, that was why most of the clientele at the Silver Spur favoured that saloon, as far as Thomas was able to gauge; so that they could lose all their money at poker. As a matter of fact, he had been toying before this night with the idea of having a fatherly chat with this particular quartet and advising them that their welcome in Fenton's Creek was wearing a little thin.

After thanking Will Flinders for keeping the three men at the scene, Sheriff Thomas dismissed him. The men at once began an ill-tempered clamour, to the effect that they were the innocent parties here and what was the law going to do about providing justice for their slain friend. Thomas did not care for being buffaloed in this fashion and he started proceedings by shutting the men up.

'I do not know,' he said slowly, 'where you fellows come from, nor how you behave when speaking to a sheriff in the usual way of things, but I tell you straight that it will not answer in my town. Any more of this shouting and I shall arrest all of you for a breach of the peace. Is that plain?'

His words had a sobering effect on the three, who were perhaps more familiar than most with ill effects of trying conclusions with lawmen. They at once shut up and waited to see what would chance next. Sheriff Thomas continued, 'I do not like crooked games in my town. It creates ill-feeling and all too often, as in the present case, results in violence. I will not have it.'

There was silence as he examined the bloody corpse that lay sprawled on the sawdust-covered floor. 'This is not a bullet wound,' said the sheriff. 'One of you tell me what happened now, but don't all of you start jabbering at once.'

Each of the three contributed to the account, leaving out that part of the affair touching upon four sevens mysteriously appearing in the dead man's hand to beat the full house which had been laid down. At the end of the tale, Thomas said, 'It is an unfortunate circumstance that your friend here has been killed, which I will freely grant. Howsoever, if you rook some stranger of his money, there is no telling how he is going to take it. Strikes me that you boys might want to go for another line of work, because this here that has happened this night is very much in the way of what you might term an occupational hazard for cardsharps.'

Sheriff Thomas ignored the furious cries which erupted at the word 'cardsharps'. He continued, 'I will certainly be investigating this crime, of that you may have no doubt. There is also the matter of a concealed weapon.' The Derringer had been found on the floor by the barkeep and handed to the sheriff. 'You fellows might not know it, but we frown on the carrying of guns which are not out in the open round here. Any of you want to claim this?' None of them did.

In the end, Thomas let the three of them leave, suspecting and also hoping that they would dig up and leave town that very night. In the event, this is just precisely what they did.

As he walked back to the office to write out a report on the night's happenings, Sheriff Thomas was not easy in his mind. This was the second murder in town in a little over a week. Then again, that very day he had received a visit from a man from Washington DC, who had letters of recommendation which asked the sheriff to cooperate with him to the best of his ability. There was seemingly some big trouble in the wind and from all that Sheriff Thomas was able to collect, his own little town was at the centre of it.

4

Almost as soon as she woke the next morning, Harriet Thorndike thought of the young man who had called at the house the previous day. Her mother would have a seizure if she heard of her daughter calling on some unknown man in a hotel and so before she made contact with him, it seemed sensible to see if it was true that Mr Wexford knew something about him. Before this, though, she was eager to read more about her uncle's life and so after breakfast, she took out the heavy ledger and deciphered another few pages of the Pig Latin.

I think that I thought in those early years much the same as many of the Indians with whom I came into contact. Whether Chiricahua or Sioux, Choctaw or Cherokee, all harboured the hope that they would one day have their own country, a land alongside that of the white people. In 1850, this was a realistic prospect. The Indian Country, as it was known then, was a vast tract of land, taking up perhaps a third of what we now call the United States. It would have made perfect sense, if only my own countrymen were not so greedy. As it was, year by year, as gold was discovered here or the Butterfield Stage wanted a new route there, or homesteaders were running out of space in this state or that, little by little the Indian Country was being nibbled away.

All I ever wanted was for the white man and the red to live side by side; each with his own nation and land. There were other white men who felt like me, but against the rapacity of others, there was not much that could be done. This is why I continued to help my friend Goyahkla by selling the gold for him and then passing on the money to his tribe. He insisted that I took enough for myself at the same time. In those first few years after we met, I was beginning to gain a name for myself as an expert on Indian affairs and even the government was consulting me on what some called the 'Indian Problem'.

So it was, that the higher I climbed in the counsels of my own people, so too did I forge stronger and stronger links with the tribes. It was not just the Chiricahua with whom I came into contact. I had many connections with the five so-called civilised tribes and it was they who seemed for a time most likely to have a country of their own; a place that all the Indians could call their homeland; somewhere free from the avarice and cruelty of the white man.

It was not a comfortable situation to be in, of course. Sometimes I felt that I was betraying my own people, but as long as they were behaving like beasts towards their red brothers, I felt that my actions were justified.

Since his late client's death, Jacob Wexford had been besieged, or so it appeared to him, by a constant stream of callers wanting to know more about the dead man's life, money and affairs. At least his niece was pleasant to look at and hear. Wexford listened to what the young woman had to say and then told her, 'You may be easy in your mind about Mr McFadden. I can vouch for him. I can tell you that he enjoyed your uncle's trust and that he has some connection with the federal government. The Bureau of Indian Affairs or some such, I believe.'

'What was his connection with my uncle?'

'That I could not say. But I can tell you that your uncle liked and trusted the man.'

'Mr Wexford,' began Harriet hesitantly, 'is there anything I should know about my uncle? That is to say, is there something which I don't know, I mean that I ought to know but nobody has told me . . . ' She tailed off, feeling uncommonly foolish.

Mr Wexford regarded her benevolently over the top of his gold-rimmed glasses. 'You had best address all questions of that nature to Mr McFadden himself, my dear. I am hardly competent to answer them.'

And with that, Harriet had to be content, as she left the attorney's office disconsolately and made her way to the Supreme Hotel; the best place to stay that Fenton's Creek could offer.

★   ★   ★

All in all, Sheriff Thomas thought, the affair at the Silver Spur could have turned out a lot worse. He intimated as much to his deputy.

'Bill my boy, it strikes me that we have not done too badly over that shooting last night.'

Bill Carter smiled back at his boss. 'I was thinking much the same thing myself. The man killed was not from our town and now his friends have dug up and gone, the case is all but concluded.'

'All we really know,' said the sheriff, 'Is that some half-breed or Spanish-looking fellow committed the crime. I have spoke to a few people who recall having seen such a person about Main Street in recent days, but nobody seems to know who he was or where he was staying. If neither the killer nor his victim came from here, then I would say that that lets us out of the cart, really.'

The two men smoked and drank coffee in companionable silence for a couple of minutes, before Carter said, 'What did that smart-looking easterner want yesterday?'

'Damned if I know. He is some big wheel in the Bureau of Indian Affairs and wondered if we had any informa-tion on the Thorndike murder. He is a special assistant to the Commissioner for Indian Affairs himself.'

'Anything which is likely to trouble us?'

'No,' said Thomas, with great satisfaction, 'I wouldn't have thought so.'

★ ★ ★

Harriet Thorndike was spared the experience of coming across as a particularly fast young woman by arriving unaccompanied at a hotel and asking about a single young man. Patrick McFadden was in the lobby when she came through the door and recognized her immediately.

'Miss Thorndike, it is a pleasure. Will you join me in the lounge for a coffee?'

She shrugged ungraciously. Harriet disliked formal settings and already felt wrong-footed by this fellow on account of having been caught out the day before in what was, to all intents and purposes, a deliberate falsehood.

McFadden led her into the plush surroundings of the Supreme's lounge, attracting the attention of a waiter without seemingly doing anything other than looking round. This fellow abased himself before the well-dressed young man and scuttled off to do his bidding. It seemed to Harriet that Mr McFadden from Washington was regarded by the staff of the Supreme as being a person of some consequence.

Once they were sitting at a table, with a silver coffee pot and a plate of cookies before them, McFadden introduced himself properly. 'Miss Thorndike,' he said pleasantly, 'I can't help but think that we got off on the wrong foot yesterday, I am sure that the fault was mine and I hope that you will forgive me and we can start again.'

This was so fair-spoken, that Harriet thought that it would be rude not to accept such an apology and in return, offer one of her own. 'I am sorry too, Mr McFadden. I was just a little scared, after what happened to my uncle. I did not know quite what to make of you, which is why I told that foolish story about Mr Wexford being present.'

McFadden took from his jacket pocket a circular piece of brass. It put

Harriet in mind of a sundial and she watched curiously as he set the disc, which was perhaps four or five inches across, onto the table in front of them. There was a round hole in the middle of the thing, about the size of a ten dollar piece. 'Tell me,' he said, 'what do you make of this?'

The girl craned her neck round to get a better view of the brass disc. 'Take it in your hands,' said McFadden. 'I want to know if it suggests anything to you.'

Harriet picked up the strange piece of metal and turned it round in her hands. She noticed that figures were engraved around the circumference of the thing. She looked closer and almost gave a gasp of understanding. Near to the circular hole was engraved a letter 'N' and there were seven little figures cut into the rest of the disc at precisely regular intervals. They were stylised representations of a fish, cat, dog, flying bird, elk, man, sun and moon. Patrick McFadden, who had been marking her closely, did not miss the slight sound she made when first she recognized the design of the thing. He said, 'I take it then that you can guess what this is for?'

'I can, if 'N' stands for north.'

'It does. I see that we may speak plainly, Miss Thorndike. Shall I say it or will you? You believe that this is what you would need to follow the map which you have doubtless by now unearthed in your uncle's house. Am I right?'

She thought for a moment or two before replying and then said, 'I suppose that a compass is placed in that hole and north lined up with the letter 'N'?'

'I believe so, yes. I have reason to suppose that your late uncle had this device made to his specifications.'

'I have not the pleasure of understanding what it is that you wish from me, Mr McFadden. You will forgive me if I speak plainly. What was your connection with my uncle?'

The young man thought about Harriet's question for a spell. Then he said, 'It's not in reason that I should ask you to trust me without telling you a little about the business. I see that. You know that your uncle was deeply interested in Indian traditions and suchlike?'

'Yes, of course. I have some of his books on that subject.'

'What you might not know is that Gabriel Thorndike was involved in more than the study of folklore. He was helping some of the tribes in a most practical way. I know some who would say that certain of his actions came perilously close to treason.'

Harriet remembered what her uncle had written about selling gold so that the Apaches could buy guns. She said nothing, but her very silence gave her away. McFadden said slowly, 'I can see that you know more about this than I realized.'

★   ★   ★

Alfred Dexter was not feeling at all happy that morning. Since he had picked up with Leon Gonsalez, three murders had been committed. In one of these, he was himself so closely mixed up that he would surely hang if his involvement became known. He knew that the prudent course of action would be simply to hightail it out of Fenton's Creek that very day and ride off in the opposite direction from that in which he might meet the Mexican again. However, the thought of large amounts of gold does strange things to men's minds. It can drive them to suicide or madness during a gold rush and even in the general way of things, such thoughts can lead sensible men to take foolish risks. Which was why Dexter was currently lying on the bed smoking, rather than riding west out of Fenton's Creek.

It was while he was putting together his plans for that day, plans which entailed passing by and perhaps even visiting the Thorndike place on some pretext or other, that there was a sharp and authoritative knock at the door. Dexter stayed still and hoped that whoever it was would just leave him in peace. There came another knock and somebody announced in a voice which sounded as though the owner would brook no foolishness, 'Open the door. This is the sheriff.'

It was ironic really. Sheriff Thomas often complained to his deputy of the reluctance displayed by the citizens of Fenton's Creek in coming forward and helping with his enquiries. Folk in the town were a sight too ready to tend to their own affairs and not volunteer information which he, as their sheriff, should know about. And now, in the one case that he had no desire at all to pursue, the owner of the Custom House saloon had beaten a path to his door to tell Thomas that he had a swarthy-looking Mexican staying at his place and he had heard the sheriff was looking for such a one in connection with the murder over at the Silver Spur.

With more than a little bad grace, Sheriff Thomas went over to the Custom House to investigate.

Dexter opened the door, trembling in fear. Although he was not in the least afeared of facing up to anything in the shooting and killing line, he had a mortal dread of being hanged. Now it looked as though somebody had linked him in with the death of the old man. Dexter's first impulse was to empty his pistol at the door and then escape through the window. The sheriff came close to death, as he stood in front of the door to that cheap room. In the end though, the man in the room decided to bluff it out. He could always start shooting later if the questions became too tricky to handle.

'You took your time opening this door,' observed Thomas. He strode to the window and peered out into the alleyway beneath. 'You wasn't perhaps giving your partner time to get clear, I suppose?'

'My partner? I don't rightly take your

meaning . . . ' began Dexter, prevaricating with what he thought was great skill.

It didn't suit Sheriff Thomas, though, who said coarsely, 'Don't screw me around. I know there was a Spanish fellow staying here with you. Where is he?'

'Oh, that fellow. He has left.'

'When did he leave?' asked the sheriff.

'Why, last night. He just came in and took all his stuff,' said Dexter. The relief he had felt when he realized that it was only Gonsalez in whom the sheriff was interested was immeasurable.

'Know where he was heading?'

'I couldn't say. He said there had been some trouble.'

'What's your name, anyway?' asked Thomas.

'Alfred Dexter. Say, what is this? You have not told me what is going on.'

Sheriff Thomas stared at the man for a second or two, sizing him up. Whatever else he had been mixed up in,

Dexter's demeanour told the sheriff that he had nothing to do with last night's killing. The man had a cocky and arrogant air; that of a man who is in the clear and knows it. 'What is his name and how do you come to be sharing a room with him?'

'That's no mystery. His name is Gonsalez and we met on the road, a way back. He wanted to go out last night. He is a gambler and drinker, you know. I have no interest in such things.'

'No,' said Sheriff Thomas dryly, 'I make no doubt that you are a regular temperance man. Let me know if your friend shows up again, you hear me?'

★　★　★

Over at the Supreme, Harriet Thorndike was doing her best to take in all the surprising things that she was being told about her Uncle Gabriel. The main point seemed to be that he was a good deal more important than she had ever suspected. According to the man from the

Bureau of Indian Affairs, the government in Washington used to consult with her uncle on matters relating to dealing with the Indians. It now appeared that they had reason to think that he had been playing a double game and helping to incite unrest among the redskins. None of this tied in in the least with what she knew of her uncle and so she thought it best just to listen to what Mr McFadden said, rather than offering her own views.

Realizing perhaps that he had not enlisted the girl's wholehearted support and that she was still being very guarded in her responses to his questions, the man from Washington decided to be as blunt as he dared. 'Have you seen the newspapers over the last few days, Miss Thorndike?'

'I have not had time for them, really. Why do you ask?'

McFadden had been carrying a paper when he met her that morning and he turned it to show her the glaring headline. It read:

The Apaches break out!!!
Great apprehension of sanguinary
conflict and rapine, as Geronimo
leads his men on the warpath
again.

'I don't understand what this has to
do with me. Or my uncle, really.'

'I will tell you. I am sure that you
know something of the troubles that
have taken place in recent years with
the Indians. You surely know about
Little Bighorn and suchlike? The Indian
Wars?'

'I am not a child,' said Harriet coldly,
'and so you need not treat me like one.'

'I'm sorry. The Indians have always
been divided. They fight more among
each other than they do against us. But
now it seems that they are hoping to
unite. The fear that we have is that the
different tribes are working to one
common end. The consequences could
be grave.'

At this, the girl laughed out loud. 'I
don't see that at all, Mr McFadden. You

are surely not suggesting that if all the Indians band together, then they will be able to take on the US army and drive us all from America? It's too absurd for words. I may not be well versed in politics or military history, but I know that much. You are trying to work up a fear about something which could never happen.'

McFadden looked at the girl with a new respect. 'That is perfectly true, Miss Thorndike. That is not, however, their aim. Does the name Sequoyah mean anything to you?'

'You will have to spell it, I'm afraid,' and when he had done so, the girl said, 'No, that brings nothing to mind.'

'It is the name of the Cherokee who devised the alphabet which is now used to write down their language. He is revered not just by the Cherokee, but among other tribes also. Those who regard the Indians as little more than savages would do well to think about the way in which a man like Sequoyah was able to devise an entire system of writing in that way. He was a great man.'

'Forgive me, Mr McFadden, but I do not quite see the way in which this connects to me and my uncle?'

'I am coming to that. There is a plan afoot for the Five Civilized Tribes in the Indian Territories to declare themselves an independent country, a sovereign state. If they do this, then they will invite all other Indians from across the country to join them. Their new country will be called Sequoyah, after the Cherokee man of learning.'

'Would that be such a bad thing?'

'It would be a disaster. It would very likely trigger off unrest in the southern states. Nobody wants to see any state seceding from the union again. You might recollect that this is how the War Between the States, the Civil War that is to say, began not all that long since.'

'What has this to do with my uncle?'

'Let's not fence any more, Miss Thorndike. Your uncle was helping the Chiricahua to sell gold. Lately, the

Apaches have come to an agreement with the leaders of the Five Civilized Tribes in the Indian Territory that they will put their gold at the disposal of the new country. We are looking at an event which could trigger the worst trouble in this country since the Civil War and I am asking for your help to stop it.'

5

The sheriff's visit had spooked Dexter some and so he decided to take a turn around the town and see if anything alarming was happening. His chief concern was that some more interest was being taken in the Thorndike place. As long as the sheriff's enquiries were limited to the murder that Gonsalez had committed the previous day, he was not that fussed. Nobody could lay that at his door. It was quite another matter with the death of Gabriel Thorndike though, in which death he had played an active part. With this object in view, he set off to stroll past the house and see if there was any sign of trouble.

Although deep inside, Alfred Dexter knew that he should just leave Fenton's Creek without any delay, still he felt bound to the spot. The lure of gold is a potent one and during a gold rush, men will become possessed of what is, in effect, almost a fever or madness. They will freeze to death or starve, simply and solely for the opportunity to pick up gold which is lying around for anybody to take for nothing. Something of this kind now gripped Dexter. So used was he to having to grub around, fighting, cheating and sometimes even killing for every dollar he could get his hands on, that Gonsalez' tale of the fabled spot where a man could just stuff his pockets with gold had entirely captivated him. This is what the lust for gold can do to a man. It makes him lose his reason and undermines his ability to think straight.

There was no sign of life at Gabriel Thorndike's house and so Alfred Dexter took what he saw as his chance. He marched right up to the front door and rapped on it smartly, like he was a regular visitor or something. There was no answer and so he went prowling round the back, to see if there was an open window or aught of that sort that he might be able to exploit. As Gonsalez had said, the dead man's relative might by now have found what they had themselves been looking for; some plan, map or set of instructions which would lead them to this Lost Dutchman's Mine.

★　★　★

'You have still not told me what you want here.' said Harriet Thorndike. 'All this about the Apaches on the warpath and a new country run by the Indians and suchlike. Where do you fit into all this?'

Patrick McFadden did not speak for a minute. He was marshalling his thoughts and also wondering how much he could safely tell this young woman and what he should conceal from her. At length, he said. 'Here is the situation in a nutshell. We none of us really know what Gabriel Thorndike was about or where his loyalties truly lay. He was a strange and complex man. What we do know is that he knew the whereabouts of the richest reef of gold in the history of America and quite possibly the entire world.'

'And I suppose,' said Harriet mischievously, 'that you are worried what will become of all this gold, now that my uncle is dead?'

'As the case now stands, anybody could find that location at any moment and claim the gold for his own. This would benefit neither the Chiricahua nor any other Indians. There would be a gold rush up on Superstition Mountain, a gold rush that would make that of 1849 look like a Sunday School picnic.

'Mr Thorndike knew this and wanted to ensure that if he died, then at least the gold there would be used for the benefit of all Indians. Still and all, he did not altogether trust me. He gave me this brass disc, which would, together with a set of instructions which he retained, make it possible for somebody to find the location of the reef.'

'What would you do with this gold? You work for the government, don't you? I suppose that the people in Washington DC would just grab it for themselves.'

'I don't work for the 'government',' he explained patiently, 'I work for the Bureau of Indian Affairs. If we can track down that gold, then it will all be used for the benefit of Indians across the nation. That is what I promised your uncle and that is what will happen. On top of that, I have been authorised by the Commissioner of Indian Affairs to offer statehood to the Indian Nation. They can have their state in eastern Oklahoma, just provided that they don't declare independence or some such foolishness.'

★ ★ ★

Dexter had not found any open window, but he had discovered the next best thing; a window that could be forced open with the assistance of the garden spade which leaned against the wall near the kitchen door. It took him only a few minutes to get the window open and then wriggle through it and so enter the house.

The house looked a mite tidier than he and Gonsalez had left it, but perhaps that was only to be expected. Dexter wandered through the rooms, looking for anything to indicate that the girl had found something which he and his partner had missed. There was nothing that he could see. After he had had a good look round on the ground floor, he went upstairs.

In one of the smaller bedrooms, Dexter found evidence of somebody staying. It was obviously the young woman that he and Gonsalez had seen at the burying ground, during the funeral of their victim. He picked up one of the dresses which lay on the bed and held it to his face. There was a sweet scent about it, which he couldn't quite place. Now that he was here, it occurred to Dexter that maybe he should take a more active role in things than had heretofore been the case. He had grown a little ticked off with the way that Gonsalez had been chivvying him around and twitting him about his lack of enterprise. How then if he could find out all they needed to know and then present the information to Gonsalez when he met him that night? He sat down on the bed and waited.

As they approached the house, Harriet Thorndike stopped one final time to remonstrate with Patrick McFadden. She said, 'Whatever you might think of me, Mr McFadden, I am perfectly capable of taking care of my own self.'

'I don't doubt it for a moment, Miss Thorndike,' he replied. 'Even so, it could do no possible harm for you to allow me to escort you home. I am not trying to crowd you into anything, you understand, but I would not mind visiting the house again in any case.'

'I have not even admitted yet that I know anything about this affair,' the girl reminded him. 'If you think that I am going to stand by while you search the house for a treasure map or something, then you are greatly mistaken. You do know that the place now belongs to me?'

'Miss Thorndike, I make not the slightest doubt that you either have, or know where is to be found, the information which I seek. I cannot make you help, if you are determined not to. But this is another matter entirely. Your uncle was murdered over this business and I would be grieved to see the same fate befall you. I will just come into the house with you and see that all is well.'

Strong-willed and independent as she was, Harriet found something more than a little pleasing about such a personable fellow looking after her in this way. She gave no sign of this though, merely shrugging in a resigned way.

★　★　★

Up in the bedroom, Alfred Dexter heard the sound of voices in the street and sneaked a look from the window. He drew back swiftly when he spotted the girl, accompanied by a capable-looking young man who appeared, to Dexter's practised eye, the sort of fellow who was apt to give trouble. He cursed under his breath and drew his pistol.

There did not appear to be anything amiss in the house when Harriet Thorndike and her companion passed through the front door. She led him into the imposing parlour and asked if he would like some coffee, to which suggestion he readily assented. A few seconds later, the girl returned, her face white. 'I think that somebody has broken in here.'

Never had she seen anybody move so fast. McFadden was on his feet in a fraction of a second and produced from somewhere a small, black pistol. Harriet had assumed that he was no more than a glorified clerk from Washington, but at this moment, she saw him in an altogether different light. He might be a civil servant, but he was also a man of action. 'Tell me what you have seen,' he said urgently.

'It is a window in the kitchen. I'll show you.'

'No,' he said sharply. 'Stay right here. I will look. Just sit tight.'

Harriet stood uncertainly in the doorway as McFadden made his way to the kitchen. From the corner of her eye she caught a flash of movement and turned in time to see an indistinct figure rushing down the stairs. 'Hey!' she cried.

At the sound of her voice, Patrick McFadden came charging from the kitchen, his gun at the ready. Whoever had come down the stairs had by this time opened the front door and was fleeing down the path. To the girl's astonishment and alarm, Mr McFadden ran to the front door and fired twice after the figure. Presumably he missed, because the shots did nothing to check the headlong progress of the man running down the street.

Dexter ran as though his life depended upon it, which was, in a very real sense, entirely the case. The bullet had missed him, but passed close enough to his head for him to hear its passage. He dived down the space between two houses and then ran on, his lungs feeling as though they would burst. He was seriously wondering if this game was worth the candle; so far it had brought him nothing but misfortune.

Back at Gabriel Thorndike's house, McFadden was not in the mood for taking 'No' for an answer. 'You cannot stay here tonight and that is flat,' he said. 'I will not debate with you about this matter. It is not to be thought of. You must stay at the Supreme tonight.'

The girl blushed at this suggestion and he added hastily, 'I'm not suggesting anything improper. Good Lord, you must see that you are in danger? I mean to book a room for you at the hotel. You can stay there until we can figure out the next move.'

To stay in a hotel paid for by a single man who until that day had been a total stranger was the most scandalous thing that Harriet Thorndike had ever heard in the whole course of her life. The colour still had not left her cheeks. She said, 'Mr McFadden, I'm very grateful and everything, but really, it won't do at all. Have you lost your mind? Think how it would look.'

'I don't give a damn how it looks,' he declared, 'I don't want you to be in danger.'

'There's no need for language of that sort,' said Harriet, a little shocked despite her modern and up-to-date opinions.

'I'm sorry. But if your sense of propriety is offended by the idea of having your hotel bill paid by a man, then I can set your mind at rest on that score. It won't be me paying, but the government. I have a pretty wide discretion over what I spend money on during this business and as far as I am concerned, you are an asset too valuable to be put at hazard.'

The girl perked up a little at that. 'Is that what you see me as, an asset?' she enquired pertly.

'Either that,' said McFadden, 'or a liability. I cannot quite make up my mind.'

*   *   *

When Sheriff Thomas heard that there had been gunfire up at the Thornton place, he felt instinctively that the young fellow from the Bureau of Indian Affairs was sure to be mixed up in the case somewhere. He set off to the Supreme, just to have a friendly word with the man about the importance of everybody recollecting whose jurisdiction was whose. Thomas did not take to the idea of some youngster from the Capitol throwing his weight around and perhaps discharging firearms on the streets.

Just as he had suspected, Patrick McFadden had been doing the shooting, as he freely admitted when the sheriff ran him to earth at the hotel. 'I'm sorry, sheriff, you are right. I should not have done it. It was hot pursuit, you know how it feels.'

Sheriff Thomas rubbed his chin thoughtfully. 'Sure I know how it feels, but I am surprised to find a clerk from Washington telling me about hot pursuit and the temptation to open fire on a fugitive. I suppose that you *are* just that; which is to say a clerk from an office?'

'I have had various positions,' said the young man vaguely. 'I am sure that you do not wish to hear my life's history. If you are worried, why not wire Washington?'

'I did so as soon as you arrived,' was the reply. 'They asked me to give you every assistance and hinted that the mission on which you are engaged is a matter of national security. Though how that connects up with old Mr Thorndike is another question entirely.'

At this moment, Harriet Thorndike arrived in the lobby where McFadden and the sheriff were talking.

'Miss Thorndike,' said the sheriff, in a voice which suggested that he was not over-pleased to see that she and the man to whom he was talking were apparently friends. 'May I ask what you are doing here?'

'Surely,' she replied, 'I have moved to the hotel for tonight at least. You said yourself that it might not be safe for me to stay at my uncle's house and I find that you are right.'

'Would either of you care,' enquired the sheriff, 'to tell me what is going on here? I do not like mysteries in my town and when they tend towards murder and gunfire, then I am apt to start getting irritable. I hope that you two are not up to some game in this town that might lead to unpleasantness.'

* * *

Alfred Dexter did not wish to be seen on the streets of Fenton's Creek in broad daylight. He had a terrible suspicion that somebody would be after pointing him out and raising a hue and cry. He did not know if either the girl or the fellow who had taken a shot at him had seen him clearly enough to identify him at a later stage. Although he was not due to ride out and meet Gonsalez until ten that night, Dexter figured that the man would probably be near the old stone shelter right now. There was nowhere else around there to lie low and the Mexican would hardly be sightseeing. He accordingly lit out east at around midday.

As he had surmised, Gonsalez was sleeping in the shelter. He was pleased to see Dexter, but annoyed when the other confessed that he had forgotten to bring any food with him. 'You think this is like a hotel here, no? That I can just ring the bell and call up a drink and so on? Is that what you believe?'

'There is no point taking that road

with me, Gonsalez,' said the other evenly. 'If you were not so quick to anger, you would not be in this fix now.'

Gonsalez grimaced. 'That at least is true. What do you find out, tell me everything.'

When Dexter had brought the Mexican up to date with events, the other man looked thoughtful and quite pleased with himself. 'It is just as I thought. The girl has found something and now she is teaming up with somebody to go up to Superstition Mountain. She knows.'

'I don't see that,' said Dexter.

'Do you not? Ach, but your brain is not so nimble as mine, perhaps.'

'Maybe not,' said Dexter, 'but at least I ain't yet a-wanted for murder in the nearest town. Having a nimble brain don't seem to have give you too much in the way of an advantage, as you might put the case.'

'The question is,' said Gonsalez, 'What are we to do now? I am almost sure of this; anybody who knows anything of the whereabouts of the gold would not give to another the information about how to get to it. You might, as we are doing, team up with some other person, but you would not say, 'Here my friend, is the map for the treasure!' What do you say?'

'You think that they are going to head off together?'

'Ah yes, that is just what I think. You know the nearest town to Superstition Mountain? It is a little place called Phoenix. That is where they will go or my name is not Leon Gonsalez.'

'Which I only have your word for anyway is the fact of it,' remarked Dexter. 'What do you want to do?'

'I want you to go back to town and see if there is any sign of the two of them making preparations to leave. My horse, it is still at the livery stable?'

'Far as I know.'

'I had to walk here last night. Ten miles in the dark. It was not pleasant. Find out what they are about and at the first sign that they are getting ready to travel, come here with my horse. We will then head to Phoenix and hope to catch up with them there before they head up to the mountains. They will surely stop in Phoenix, if only for a night or two.'

By a curious coincidence, at the very moment that Leon Gonsalez was delivering himself of this opinion, Patrick McFadden and Harriet Thorndike were actually talking about Phoenix. There was, however, a great divergence of views between them about the possibility of their visiting that town together.

'It is not to be thought of,' said McFadden, appalled. 'I cannot agree to anything of the sort.'

What had precipitated this vehement statement was quite simple. Gabriel Thorndike's niece having practically admitted that she was in possession of a guide to the Chiricahua gold, the man from the Bureau for Indian Affairs had suggested that she hand over to him the information and he would then make the necessary arrangements. This did not suit the young woman at all. She still did not entirely trust the man sitting opposite her at lunch and although she stopped short of saying as much to his face, it was plain that she was not about to provide him with all the required clues to find the gold.

'Your uncle trusted me,' said McFadden. 'I do not think that it is for you to try now to frustrate his purpose.'

'He can't have trusted you all that much,' she observed saucily, 'else he would have given you the instructions that go with that piece of hardware.'

'Well I guess he trusted me a deal more than he did you,' responded the young man. 'He did not tell you anything of this matter, is that not so? Come, Miss Thorndike, be sensible. You are obstructing me in the execution of my duty.'

'Are you a policeman?' she enquired curiously.

'Not exactly,' was the evasive reply.

'It seems to me,' said Harriet, 'that we have reached what the French would call an *impasse*. The only solution is for us to travel together to this mountain and see what we can do when we get there.'

It was absolutely infuriating. Geronimo and his men were already heading towards Superstition Mountain. The rumour was that Sitting Bull was about to announce to his people that the Sioux should all head for the Indian Territories, ready for the declaration of independence of Sequoyah; wherever one looked, there were signs of unrest among all the different tribes. Some even said that a prophet had arisen from the Cherokee, one who was possessed by the spirit of Sequoyah. And here was this foolish girl, delaying him as though he were just trying to fix up a barbecue or picnic or something of that sort.

Even as he was overwhelmed with irritation at the false position in which he was placed, McFadden could not help admiring the way that the old man had fixed things up. He wasn't about to entrust the secret of that gold to one person, but intended always that the two people he trusted with it should have to work in tandem.

'What would your mother say, if she heard that you were going on to Phoenix in the company of a man you hardly knew?' asked McFadden cunningly. 'Is this what she has raised you to; gadding about the country so without any sort of a chaperone?'

'You tend to your own affairs and leave me to look after my own,' she responded sharply. 'Either we go together or before God I shall travel to Phoenix by myself and walk up that mountain if need be. I am not returning to Boston until this business is settled and you needn't think it for a minute.'

'It is not an easy journey. The railroad does not run to Phoenix. It would mean two days travel by stage. I do not think you would care for such a thing. You would get mighty sweaty and dusty.'

'Listen,' she said, with more force

than politeness, 'if you want to get to that gold this side of Thanksgiving, you had best resign yourself to going along with me. Otherwise, it's no go.'

'All right,' he said, defeated, 'but don't start crying for your mother once we are on our way. I do not think you know what you are letting yourself in for.'

6

Harriet had brought her uncle's book with her to the Supreme and after lunch she relaxed in her room and while digesting the meal, lay on the bed and read another few pages.

It was Goyahkla who first told me that the only security for the Indians would be when they had their own country, where they could be free of the white-eyes and their interference. I remonstrated when first he said this, telling him that he had his own country already; the United States. He stared at me and said moodily, 'That is the white-eyes' nation, not ours. The white-eyes want us to vanish, so that they can steal the rest of the land.'

The Chiricahua were raiding and trying to drive back the white men who seemed determined to overrun their lands. If they had not had the rifles which the sale of the sun's blood enabled them to buy, then it would have gone even worse for them. But every year, more and more settlers were coming from the east and each time I visited the Apaches, the areas where they could roam were smaller and smaller. It was the same with all the tribes that I knew. Everywhere I went, the white men were taking over and it looked to me, as well as to the Indians, that the white man would not be happy until he had gobbled up all the land and taken it for himself.

Things got far worse during the War Between the States. Both sides took the opportunity that the war presented to attack the Indians and drive them further from their ancient hunting grounds. Terrible massacres, like that at Sand Creek, made their intentions clear. The reservations onto which the Indians were being driven were being reduced in size all the *time, until in the end they were little better than prison camps.*

After the war ended, I met with leaders from various tribes and listened to their complaints. By this time, the government in Washington was asking me when they wanted to know anything about the 'Indian Problem'. They naturally thought that I was on their side and the way they talked of my friends in the tribes made me sick at heart. I knew then that I did not owe those barbarians anything and that it was my moral duty to help the Indians to the best of my ability; even if this should mean working against my own country's interests.

She closed the book and laid it to one side. Harriet felt a little shocked at what she had read. It was all but being a confession to treason against the United States. Her uncle had been working with the Indians to fight his fellow countrymen and helped supply them with the weapons that would be used to kill both soldiers and civilians. She had read accounts of the savagery of Indian attacks; that her Uncle Gabriel was somehow mixed up in this was a terrible revelation to her. She did not think that she would be sharing these insights with Mr McFadden any time soon.

★ ★ ★

If he had been able to find out where the directions to the Chiricahua gold were to be found, then it is entirely possible that Patrick McFadden would have just taken them and left Harriet Thorndike behind in Fenton's Creek. As it was, he did not know if there even now existed a map or list of instructions or anything at all solid. Perhaps the girl had memorised the damned thing by now and burnt the original. There seemed to be little choice at the moment, but to allow her to tag along; at least as far as Phoenix. Maybe there he would be able to engineer an opportunity to search her luggage or something.

★ ★ ★

Once he got back to Fenton's Creek, Dexter went straight to his room at the Custom House and locked himself in. He lay down on the bed and tried to reason the thing through, with the aid of a good deal of tobacco. Gonsalez was probably right and the girl and that slick-looking fellow she had been with were almost certainly going to be heading towards this mountain and its lost mine. They must have some kind of map, though, and it was really going to be a matter of waiting until they were out in the open and then waylaying them and finding it.

Coaches passed through Fenton's Creek and Dexter supposed that the thing to do would be to find out when the next one east was due to leave the town. He and Gonsalez could just ride off and be fairly sure of getting to Phoenix either before or just a little behind the stage.

★ ★ ★

All things considered, Harriet Thorndike was feeling pretty pleased with herself. This was the first long trip that she had made away from her mother and on her own. She intended to make the most of it. After all, she was now the owner of a substantial property and if she wished to, she supposed that she could even move to Fenton's Creek and take up residence in her uncle's house. As a young woman of property, well, if she wanted to visit some nearby town, she could not see whose affair it was but her own. She was not, after all, a child any more. Besides, the thought of taking a trip with that fellow who was working for the government appealed to her romantic nature. It was as good as a play to think of the two of them sharing a stage to Phoenix.

★ ★ ★

Although the reservation which lately Geronimo and his warriors had left was over two hundred miles from Fenton's Creek, this did not stop the townsfolk there from feeling the pleasurable chill of fear, at the thought of hundreds of crazed Apaches descending on their homes to wreak bloody havoc. The last time Geronimo went on his travels, the self-same thing happened. The army went in pursuit of him and corralled him and his men back to the barren strip of land that the government had set aside for his people.

The reservation at San Carlos lay to the east of Phoenix and since nobody really knew where Geronimo was headed, those running the stage were a mite chary of maintaining their regular schedules. When McFadden went to the offices of the company that had taken over the route from Butterfield's, he found that there was some doubt as to the stage running in that direction at all; at least until the army had secured the area. Nevertheless, he purchased two tickets for the coach that would, it was hoped, be departing Fenton's Creek for Phoenix the following day.

★   ★   ★

About the only way that Alfred Dexter could find of disguising his appearance, just in case the old man's niece or her male companion had managed to get a good look at him as he had rushed from the house, was by changing his shirt and pulling his hat down low over his eyes. Had he but known it, this gave him a most singular, not to say downright sinister, aspect. He drew attention at once, as a man who was obviously desirous of concealing his identity. He walked in this conspicuous way to the offices of the stage, keeping his head bent low so that passers-by could catch barely a glimpse of his face.

The clerk at the office had nothing much to do that day, most folk having delayed any travelling until the present emergency with the Indians had passed. Dexter slouched into the place and asked, 'Is the stage running to Phoenix still?'

'That is,' said the clerk, bored and glad to find a chance of breaking the monotony of the day with a little friendly conversation with a fellow being, 'by way of being a debateable point, if you take my meaning.'

'I don't,' said Dexter gruffly. 'Is the stage running or not?'

'Well,' said the man, 'that is theoretically the case, yes. But whether it will arrive tomorrow is very much open to question. If it does, then yes, we will be running the regular service to Phoenix.'

'Couple of friends of mine said they might be going that way,' said Dexter. 'Anybody bought tickets for that coach yet?'

'Why yes, I sold two tickets to Phoenix not an hour since. Is your friend a smartly dressed party, looks well-off and sounds like an easterner? Travelling with a lady, it seems.'

'That's the ones. What time is that there stage of yours due to set off tomorrow? Allowing, that is, that it does leave?'

'It should get here at about midday, God willing.'

Now Alfred Dexter might not have been the fastest thinker who ever walked the earth, but he could see well enough what was needful under these given circumstances. He and Gonsalez would not be able to outride the coach unless they had a start on it. The way of it must be that they would steal a march on the stagecoach by setting off this very night, when he took the Mexican's horse to him where he was hiding out.

If they started tonight, then they would be sure to hit Phoenix before the stage and it would only be a matter of hanging round the depot and then picking up their marks when they arrived.

★ ★ ★

'The clerk says that there are no stages at all running to Phoenix,' said Patrick McFadden mendaciously, 'at least while the current emergency lasts.'

'Oh, what a nuisance,' said Harriet, 'I was so looking forward to a trip.'

'Looking forward to a trip? Miss Thorndike, you will forgive my remarking that you do not seem able fully to grasp the gravity of this situation. Things are moving fast and if I don't secure that goldfield in the next week, there is no telling what might result.'

The girl said nothing, but regarded him with a kind of mulish obstinacy which irked him greatly. 'Come, Miss Thorndike, I will appeal to your patriotism, if nothing else. We are facing a situation where what is practically a state of the union is about to secede. It will be like the Civil War all over again. Will you be the one who allows this disaster to occur?'

'What do you suggest?'

'If the stagecoach does not run, then I can make the journey fast enough by horse. If you give me the information that I need, then I can act alone. I have told you already, this is what your uncle would have wanted.'

Harriet looked at him, her face expressionless. She said, 'I don't rightly trust you, Mr McFadden. I think that you are trying to ditch me. What if I go now to the office of the stage and ask them about this business, that is to say if the stage to Phoenix will be running?' She saw the irritation in his face and crowed triumphantly. 'I knew it! I just knew it, you are not being truthful with me. How can you expect me to trust you when you can tell a lie to me so easily?'

'I am trying to protect you,' he said a little stiffly.

'No,' cut in the girl, 'you are trying to trick me and have everything your own way. Well it will not answer. If we don't go to Phoenix together, then you can take your chunk of metal and try your luck with that on your own. It won't help you, though. The route is circuitous and without what I know, you will never find the place.'

*　*　*

That evening, two pairs of people were engaged in two very different courses of action; the one being a good deal more pleasurable than the other. Alfred Dexter was leading Gonsalez' horse east out of town with a view to joining up with his partner and riding like the devil for Phoenix. There had been a little unpleasantness at the livery stable, the owner being unwilling to release the Mexican's horse without first notifying the sheriff. This was the last thing that Dexter wished to see happening.

When once the fellow at the livery stable cottoned on to the fact that here was a man eager to avoid any dealings with the law, he saw his own edge and worked hard to exploit it for all that it was worth.

'Sorry, fellow,' he said, in a voice which suggested the very opposite emotion, 'I can't go against what Sheriff Thomas told me. I have to make out a report to him if anybody comes for this here horse.'

'Don't be a fool, man,' said Dexter, most injudiciously for his purpose. 'I am paying you the bill. Where is your profit otherwise? You think the owner of the horse will return to pay you? He is wanted for murder, as perhaps you know.'

As far as the other man was concerned, this made it a racing certainty that the fellow trying so hard to get the horse out of his stable was up to no good. The only question was, how much would he be prepared to pay to avoid a lot of awkward enquiries? The answer to this riddle was $20, which was all that he was able to gouge out of Dexter in the way of a bribe. For this, he agreed to surrender the horse and keep his mouth shut afterwards and pretend that the beast had escaped through its own efforts.

As he saddled up and mounted his own horse and prepared to lead Gonsalez' creature out into the night, Dexter leaned down and said to the man running the livery stable, 'You are lucky that I am in an amiable frame of mind this day. Otherwise, who knows what might have befallen you.'

The man smiled up at him, saying, 'You have a nice time now, you hear what I say? Good doing business with you.' He would give it an hour or two and then see if there was anything in the nature of a reward for informing the sheriff about what had happened.

★　★　★

It made Harriet feel very grown-up and important to be having dinner at the Supreme in the company of such a handsome man as Patrick McFadden. He had evidently resigned himself to being stuck with her, at least for the next few days, and looked to her to be making the best of a bad job. As they had their soup, she said, 'I still can't make out what you are so afraid of with a few Indians heading over to Oklahoma. So what if the Apache or Sioux move into the Indian Territories? They won't be bothering us any more then, will they?'

'Over the last year or so,' said McFadden slowly, 'I have visited a number of reservations and also spoken to Indians living in cities and towns. Everywhere, it is the same. The one name on everybody's lips is Sequoyah. For the first time that anybody can recall, the Indians are unified. They think that their time has come.'

'Well why should they not have their own little bit of land?' the girl enquired. 'It wouldn't do any harm to us, would it?'

'It would set a mighty poor precedent. The Indian Territories, that is to say the area which they hope will become this Sequoyah, is right next door to Arkansas and Texas. They will be watching how we deal with this. If we let Sequoyah come into being and act like they are independent, then some of those southern states will be up to the same game. Just as they did in 1861, you know. There's the very real fear in Washington that this could set a match to the powder keg and we'll next be having men calling for states' rights and all the rest of it. It is not to be thought of. Nobody will be leaving the union.'

'What did my uncle think that you would do, if, that is, you could find and claim the gold on Superstition Mountain?'

'First off is where he wanted to ensure that all the money from that gold would be used for the benefit of the Indians. That's all right, I have a cast-iron assurance of that from my superiors. But secondly, I think that Gabriel Thorndike wanted the Indians to have a state of their own, meaning one within the union. That's all right too. Oklahoma is aiming to become a state in the next few years and there is no reason why the Indian Territories could not apply for statehood at the same time. They could even call themselves Sequoyah, if that is what they wished. If that happened, then I make no doubt that the Apache gold up on Superstition Mountain would be used for their good.'

It all sounded very plausible and Harriet wanted to believe that McFadden was an honest man, but he was only one man. Who knew what the government in Washington really wanted? And when all was said and done, she did not even know if her uncle had really given him the brass disc that he was carrying. How did she know that he had not just stolen it? It was a riddle, to which she did not seem likely to find the answer in a hurry.

★   ★   ★

While Harriet Thorndike and Patrick McFadden were foxing with each other in this wise, Alfred Dexter was handing the horse over to Gonsalez. Lord knew that Leon Gonsalez was a mean one at the best of times, but after sleeping rough and being without provisions or even water for the best part of twenty-four hours had made him as dangerous as a rattler. The light-hearted veneer had all worn away, leaving visible just a desperate killer who would clearly stop at nothing.

'Tell me again,' said Gonsalez, as he tore ravenously at the bread and meat which Dexter had brought him, 'are you sure that the girl and this other will be going to Phoenix?'

'No,' said Dexter imperturbably, 'I ain't sure. But it seems our best bet. You know that the Apache are rising? Geronimo is out raising hell again. Never mind those two getting through on the stage, we will have a lively time of it ourselves if we run into those braves.'

'Apaches? These are Chiricahua. They are worse than the devil for hating men such as me.'

'Why you especially? What have you done to upset them?'

'The Chiricahua hate all Mexicans.'

'Why so?'

'Ach, does it matter? Well then, at one time we hunted the Chiricahua like animals. The governor of Chihuahua paid a bounty on scalps of Apache, especially Chiricahua Apache. One day, the army came across a camp of women and children. The men were away hunting. The Mexican soldiers killed some and took others to sell into slavery. When he that you call Geronimo returned, he found that they had killed his mother, his wife and his three children. From that day on, he has never missed a chance to kill Mexicans.'

'I don't rightly know that I blame him,' said Dexter.

'If we are to ride, then we ride. I do not wish to sit here gossiping with you like old women.'

'Suits me well enough, Gonsalez. You are no great shakes at this conversation business.'

The two men rode west as night fell, being careful to skirt far round Fenton's Creek as they headed towards Phoenix.

★　★　★

McFadden had to concede that, irritating and obstinate as she was, Harriet Thorndike made a most agreeable dinner companion. She was lively, witty and good-humoured. He felt a twinge of regret that he had not encountered her under more congenial circumstances. She might be a damned nuisance from a purely business point of view, but as a woman she was definitely attractive.

As they ate the fish, he asked the girl, 'How did you come to spend so much time with your uncle when you were little?'

'My father was killed in the war. My mother took it ill and for a space she could not care for me. She was bowed down with grief and I think that her mind gave way under the burden of it all. So I was packed off here. Uncle Gabriel was the most wonderful person you can imagine for a child to live with. I know that you might have thought him dry and stuffy, but he was just shy, really. My times here were the happiest in my childhood.'

'It gives me a different slant on your uncle,' said McFadden. 'I was sent here from time to time to gauge his views on various matters and I used also to correspond with him. He never struck me as a man who would be very good with children, I must say.'

'How well really did you know Uncle Gabriel? Please tell me honestly. I know that there is more to you than meets the eye, but I loved him so and I would like to know more about his life in recent years.'

'My relation with your uncle was purely business, Miss Thorndike. He would tell us what the Indians' view was on this or that development. He always told me straight, at least as far as anybody can judge. But I have no doubt that he was also playing some game of his own. I would not be overly surprised to learn that he loved the Indians more than his own people and only told us enough so that we would keep coming back to consult him. He certainly gained much information from me and the Bureau of Indian Affairs in general, while these exchanges were taking place. I wonder if he did not pass this on to his Indian friends. Truth to tell, I would not be too overcome with amazement to learn that it was your uncle who helped put the whole idea of Sequoyah into their heads.'

'I had no idea that he was so important.'

'He was important enough,' said the young man grimly. 'If there is a general Indian uprising, something like Little Bighorn across the whole of the west, then you will see how important he was, I'll warrant.'

★ ★ ★

The moon was high in the sky as Leon Gonsalez and Alfred Dexter rode south-west at a brisk canter. If they were to beat the stage into Phoenix, then they would need to maintain a pretty smart pace, snatching sleep only for a few hours at a time. The stage would be changing horses at several points on the journey, but Gonsalez and Dexter had only the same horses to carry them the whole, entire distance. It would be a fine-cut thing as to whether it would be they or the stagecoach that reached Phoenix first.

'What do you purpose when or if we pick up their trail in Phoenix?' asked Dexter.

'They will stay in the town for a night or two and then head out to the mountain. It is not far from the town. We must set a watch upon them and be ready to follow at a distance. If we can catch them unawares, when nobody else is near at hand, then we should do well enough. One way or another, I think that we can persuade them to tell us all that we wish to know.'

★ ★ ★

As she headed up to her room, Harriet turned suddenly and walked back to where Mr McFadden was standing. She went up to him and without any warning, kissed him on the cheek. 'Thank you for a lovely evening,' she said, 'and thank you, too, for talking about my uncle. I look forward to our vacation tomorrow.' With that, she turned and walked straight off.

Patrick McFadden stood as though transfixed to the spot. His hand reached up and touched his cheek where the girl's lips had brushed it. Then he shook his head and smiled. Vacation, indeed! Mind, if he was honest about it, he too was looking forward to spending more time in Harriet Thorndike's company and the fact that it was strictly business did not in any way detract from the pleasure that he felt at the prospect of sharing a coach with her for a day or two.

7

Before sleeping, Harriet wanted to read a little more of her uncle's book. Much of it was taken up with a lot of stuff that she did not really understand. There were many Indian names, and information about places of which she had never heard. She skipped those sections and moved forward. Choosing a page just before the end of the book, she at once realized that she had struck gold, as you might say. Almost the first word on that page was CFADDENMAY. It seemed at least that Mr McFadden had been telling the truth about having some kind of dealings with her uncle Gabriel.

There is a new man over at the Bureau of Indian Affairs. A young fellow called McFadden. Unless I miss my guess, he has been seconded from the army or police or some such. He took the trouble to come calling on me in person and I found him to be a polite, honest and trustworthy enough man. I wonder though, if he knows what a set of rascals and scamps those at the Bureau are in general. Worst of the bunch is that so-called Commissioner for Indian Affairs.

The older I get, the more I value people for their individual qualities, rather than the office they work for or even their race. Take Goyahkla. After all the years I have known him, I can say that here is a man that I would trust more than anybody I have ever known. But that is because of the man himself; not the tribe or race to which he belongs. It is the same with young Patrick McFadden. Him I trust, but not the precious bureau which he represents. Nevertheless, I think that I might be able to come to some accommodation with him about Superstition Mountain. If the plans now being laid come to fruition, then

Goyahkla tells me that the Chiricahua would have no objection to the gold being used to support an entire Indian Nation. I have similar assurances from a dozen other leaders, including Sitting Bull. At long last, Sequoyah is about to become a reality.

I have been in correspondence with colleagues in England, Mexico and France. They all feel sure that once the exiles are safely gathered to the territories and the declaration made, then their countries will agree to recognize Sequoyah swiftly. I am confident that if this happens, then neither the Bureau of Indian Affairs, nor even the government in Washington will be able to do anything further. It is one thing to send the army chasing a lot of ragged Indians when they are rampaging across what we are pleased to call 'white' districts. Imagine though, the Indians in their own territory raising a flag and declaring themselves to be a sovereign nation. How would it look if the US army were sent in to crush such *a new young country, to strangle it at birth? With our history of the War of Independence, the Battle of the Alamo and so forth, it would make America look like an oppressor. No, once Sequoyah is declared, then it will be here to stay.*

Like any prudent man though, I have a reserve in place, lest this first plan should fail. You could call the declaration of the independence of the Indian Nation an ideal. I think though, that we should be prepared if necessary to settle for less; although nothing less than full statehood for Sequoyah.

Harriet wondered if she should tell Mr McFadden of the contents of her uncle's book. He had, as far as she could make out, guessed most of it already and there might be no harm now in letting him see that he was right.

Then again, she did not really know how she herself felt about this notion of an independent country for the Indians. Coming, as she did, from Boston, she had seen few Indians in real life and had always felt a little uneasy about them. Despite spending a large chunk of her childhood living with Gabriel Thorndike, Harriet had still absorbed the commonly held view of the redskins; that they were savages who spent most of their time scalping men and raping women. What would a country of such people be like? Would it be a menace to those who lived as neighbours to them?

The girl could not come up with any clear answer to questions of this sort and so changed into her nightgown, climbed into bed and slept soundly until the morning.

* * *

Gonsalez had said at sunup that they should take a break and let the horses have their rest. He and Dexter lit a fire and brewed up some coffee in Dexter's mess-tin. 'Tell me,' said Dexter, 'why do they call this place a mine if, as you say, the gold is just lying around waiting to be collected up?'

'How do I know the foolish ways of men?' asked Gonsalez. 'I think, though, that seeing the great seam of gold near to the surface, one of these men brought up supplies, with the idea of digging down into the earth to follow the reef of gold. I heard that this was what caught the attention of the Apache. They saw mules laden with pit-props and so on labouring up the sacred mountain.'

'And what will we do, if, that is, we find the place? Do you say that we should stake a legal claim to the area?'

'That depends what we find. If there is any staking of claims, my friend, then it would have to be in your name and not mine. I am not a citizen of your wretched country.'

Dexter filed away this useful information for use at a later date. He might not have the sharpness of intellect that the Mexican displayed, but he could certainly file a claim. He had also in the past shot a fellow in the back when he had found it necessary to do so in order to protect his own interests. He had done it before and would not hesitate to do it again should the need arise. But in the meantime, he and Gonsalez needed each other. It was all well and good building mansions in the sky, but first they must find this treasure and figure out how to get it down from the mountain. There was a little way to go yet before he would be thinking about the neatest way to dissolve this partnership.

★   ★   ★

At breakfast that day, Harriet was determined to make up for that impulsive kiss by being a little distant and cool with Mr McFadden. She was horrified at herself for having behaved in such a forward way and was remembering with shame the way that she and her friends talked about girls who 'threw themselves' at men. For his part, the man from the Bureau of Indian Affairs was particularly polite; to the point where it verged upon being formal. 'I trust that you slept well, Miss Thorndike?' he enquired.

'I did, Mr McFadden. I am obliged to you.'

It was as though both young people were a little nervous about what had happened and were alarmed about what it could all mean.

Back at her uncle's house, with McFadden accompanying her for safety's sake, Harriet packed her trunk. At the last moment, she popped into it a .45 revolver that she had come across in a drawer in her uncle's desk. It seemed like the sort of thing which might prove useful at some point. There had been a box of ammunition for it and she popped that into her trunk as well. Then the two of them went to the stagecoach office and found that the clerk there had received a wire that the stage was on its way and would certainly be running to Phoenix that day. Arrangements were made for both her trunk and that of Mr McFadden to be collected and brought to the office.

Before leaving Fenton's Creek, Patrick McFadden wanted to have a final few words with Sheriff Thomas. He left Harriet at the Supreme and made his way to the sheriff's office. Thomas was not overjoyed to see him. 'Why, Mr McFadden,' he said, 'I thought that you would have left town by now. I am sure that our little place is not lively enough for a fellow like you, used to Washington and so on.'

'You don't much care for me, do you, Sheriff?' asked McFadden.

'I am sure that you are a fine enough man in your private capacity,' said the sheriff, 'but you are the sort of man who only seems to appear when there is trouble afoot. I don't say that you have made the trouble, but you are mixed up in it some way or the other.'

'Well then, you will be glad to hear that I am leaving in a couple of hours. I shall be taking Miss Thorndike with me when I go, so that will be another weight off your mind.'

'The devil you are! Do you mind telling me what you are about with that young lady?'

'She is not a minor; I can't see that you have any official interest in her movements.'

'You are, as I have already remarked, a man who is often at the centre of the cyclone, as you might put it. That is your business. I don't like to see a respectable young lady like that dragged into danger.'

McFadden gave a short and ironic laugh. 'If anybody is being dragged anywhere, then the boot is all on the other foot, sheriff. I did not want her trailing along with me. She has railroaded me into this business.'

Sheriff Thomas looked thoughtfully at the young man. 'I would not have said,' he observed, 'that you are the sort of fellow to be railroaded by anybody. Where are you going, anyway?'

'Phoenix.'

'I hear that the Apaches are on the warpath. Should you be letting a girl like that run the risk of being caught on the road in that way?'

'Well, sheriff, as to the first of those points, I might remind you that I am special assistant to the Commissioner of Indian Affairs and perhaps in a better way of judging such things as touch upon the dangers from Apaches than is perhaps the case with a small town sheriff. Then again, Miss Thorndike will have me to take care of her. Whatever the danger, she will be as safe as though she were at home in bed. Anywise, don't be looking for us for the next week or so, because we will be away for at least that long.'

It would be stretching the truth beyond breaking point to say that the two men parted on amicable terms.

The news coming across the wires was far from reassuring. In all parts of the country, the reservations were boiling over like disturbed ant-hills. It was not only the Apaches living on the

151

San Carlos reservation who were moving out. The same thing was apparently taking place with the Mescalero reservation, two hundred miles to the east of San Carlos. There was no looting, or attacks on isolated farmhouses of the sort that often followed such upheavals. Instead, there were stories of peaceful columns of Indians beginning the trek on foot towards the Indian Territories.

★ ★ ★

There were only two other passengers in the stage, which was so unusual as to be the theme of general remark. The unwritten rule was, 'Always room for one more', with many stages having people crammed inside and also hanging on the roof and sometimes from the sides. To have a stagecoach with a mere four passengers was luxury indeed.

Apart from Harriet and Patrick McFadden, there was an elderly looking man with a neatly trimmed moustache and a military bearing which hinted at a past career in the army. The other member of the party was a taciturn man in his forties, who answered any enquiry with either 'Yes' or 'No' and nothing more. It seemed to Harriet that he used either word more or less at random. For example, when they were taking their seats in the coach, Harriet chanced to tread on his foot and at once said, 'Oh, I do beg your pardon,' to which this individual replied, 'Yes.' Later, when she asked if he travelled much, he said, 'No.' and not a single word more. After a space, she gave him up as a bad job.

McFadden soon fell into conversation with the older man, who was, it seemed, a veteran of both the Mexican War and also various incidents in the Indian Wars. They knew some of the same places and also, from what Harriet could make out, they had mutual acquaintances in Washington. The older man did not ask many questions of Mr McFadden, but it was pretty plain that he saw him as a man of consequence, despite the great gap in their ages.

'I mind, sir,' said the old man, 'that you have had some considerable dealings with Indians?'

'That is so, yes. I am currently attached to the Bureau of Indian Affairs.' To Harriet, this was an odd way of stating the case. Not, 'I work for the Bureau', but rather, 'I am currently attached.' This confirmed what she had thought all along, that there was more to the man than his just being a clerk in some government department.

* * *

By the time the stage left Fenton's Creek, Gonsalez and Dexter were well ahead of it. They were riding not on the road itself, but roughly parallel to it. The land hereabouts was dusty and dry, but pretty easy on horses. The two men were alternating trotting with canters, so that their mounts did not get too winded. While they were trotting, Gonsalez said, 'What would you have been doing now, had we not met, I mean?'

Dexter shrugged. 'Carried on with a few hold-ups, I reckon. I am a man who always finds one way or another to make a few dollars.'

'Have you ever killed a man?'

Dexter reined in his horse and waited until Gonsalez had done the same. 'Why do you ask me this question?' he said.

His partner laughed. 'No reason. But then again, if I am working with a man on something like this, I need to know that he will not fail me at the critical moment.'

'Don't you set mind to that, Gonsalez,' said Dexter dryly, 'I am not a man to hold back from killing, not if it is needful. Yes, is the answer to your question. I have killed more than one man.'

'What about women?'

'Killing a man is one thing. I would have to think carefully before carrying

155

out murder on women or children.'

Gonsalez spurred on his horse, calling back over his shoulder, 'Come, we are losing time. We must ride while we talk.'

Once they were riding side by side, Gonsalez spoke again. 'I do not waste words on foolish talk to no purpose. You should know this of me by now. Here is what I propose. We follow those two, the man and woman, out to Superstition Mountain, when once they leave Phoenix. Then we will attack them and render them helpless, just like the old man back in Fenton's Creek. Afterwards, we will question them and when we have found out all that we require, then — tcheeek.' He made a sound and gesture of somebody having his or her throat cut.

'That is fine by me,' said Dexter stolidly. 'I do not mind killing a woman if there is a reason for it. You need not doubt that I shall play my part.'

★ ★ ★

The stage was due to take a little over twenty-four hours to reach Phoenix, which would mean sleeping while it was moving. Harriet wondered how this would feel. The idea of sleeping while sitting upright and still wearing one's day clothes was by way of being a novelty for her.

Harriet Thorndike had never been on a stagecoach and she had rather expected the experience to be much like travelling on a railroad train, only perhaps somewhat less smooth. In fact, she found the rolling movement made her feel a little sick after a time. As the journey continued, she began to feel more and more unwell. Desperate to avoid admitting to Mr McFadden that she felt like throwing up, Harriet recollected vaguely that she had once heard that it helped under these circumstances to keep the gaze fixed upon the horizon. Since she had a seat by the window, this proved easy to do and she at once began to feel a little better. So it was that being the only passenger constantly looking out of the window, she was the first to spot the party of riders who were keeping pace with the coach and riding along about a mile and a half to one side.

'Who do you think they are, over yonder?' Harriet asked Patrick McFadden.

'Where?' he replied. After a second or two of getting his eyes accustomed to the distance, McFadden said, 'They look like Indians. I should not fret, they are not coming this way.'

But Harriet observed that he was keeping a watchful eye upon the group of riders and that he had a worried look upon his face. He still engaged in desultory conversation with the old man, but it was clear that his mind was now occupied with the view from the coach window.

About twenty minutes after she had first spotted them, Harriet began to think that the men were nearer to the coach than they had at first been. McFadden was evidently of the same opinion, because he suddenly stood up and leaned right out of the window. He leaned out so far that Harriet was afraid that he might fall and agonised as to whether it would be quite the thing for a well-brought-up young lady to hang on to a gentleman's belt to stop him plunging to his death beneath the wheels of a speeding coach.

The girl need not have worried, because McFadden seemed perfectly at ease in the position that he had placed himself. She heard him shouting up to the driver and his mate, 'Ahoy there!' She could only hear one side of the conversation and was hugely alarmed to hear McFadden ask, 'What armament are you carrying there?' There was an indistinct response and then he said, 'I mean what guns are you carrying? Rifles, shotguns?'

By the time her travelling companion was back in his seat, there was no doubt whatsoever in Harriet's mind that the riders had moved closer to the coach. They were still heading in the same direction, but were approaching the stagecoach at a shallow angle. It looked to her as though they meant to intercept them at some point.

The old gentleman had picked up immediately that something was amiss. 'Trouble?' he asked.

'It could be,' said McFadden, 'I don't know. I see that you are carrying, sir.' This to the dark complextioned man, who said,

'Yes.'

'What about you, sir?' he said to the white-haired gentleman, 'Do you have a gun with you?'

'Yes I do. I have it here in my pocket. I have not travelled without a firearm these forty years or more. What's to do?'

'There is a bunch of riders moving slowly towards us. There are about a dozen of them and I don't know what they mean to do.'

'Indians?' asked the old man.

'Yes. I think that they are Mescaleros. Something like Apache, but a little different.' McFadden turned to the other passenger and asked, 'Do you know aught about Indians, sir?'

'No,' said the other.

'What I propose is this. My friend here, this young lady, had best move over to the other side of the coach, so that if there is any fighting, she is not in the line of fire. If things get a little hot, Miss Thorndike, you may have to lie on the floor. You two men have no objection to taking part in the defence, if it comes to that?'

'I have not been in a skirmish for some years,' said the older of the two men, 'but I'm game for it.'

'What about you, sir?' asked McFadden of the younger man.

'Yes,' he replied.

★   ★   ★

The two men who had left Fenton's Creek before the stage were continuing at a steady pace. They were not going so fast as to wear out their horses, but neither were they dawdling. If they had been on foot, they would have been moving at what is sometimes known as 'scout's pace'; that is to say a hundred paces walking and then a hundred paces at a run. With horses, this translated into alternating walking, trotting and cantering.

Gonsalez seemed to be in an affable mood that day. Perhaps it was being clear of Fenton's Creek and the apprehension of being called to account for the man whose throat he had cut at the gambling house. At any rate, he was more cheerful than Dexter had seen him before.

'If I did not know you better,' said Dexter, 'I might think that you were in a good mood.'

'Ach,' said Gonsalez, 'what is this 'good mood' that you Anglos are always talking of? I am alive, I have the prospect of soon being rich. That is enough for me. Nobody is chasing me, I am free and the sun is shining.'

'Which is as much as to say,' said

162

Dexter, 'that I was right and you are in a good mood.'

'Yes, if you like. What about you? You never seem to have this famous 'good mood'. I don't recollect that I have once seen you smile since we picked up together. Why is that?'

'I've nought to smile about, I guess.'

'What then? You are alive, you are healthy and free. What more would you have?'

'No wonder,' said Dexter, 'that you people have not made a mighty nation of Mexico, if all it needs to make you content is a bit of good weather. You need to strive more.'

8

The Indians were now no more than a few hundred yards from the stagecoach. They had made no hostile move, but set against that was the fact that they could have no reason to be keeping pace in this way, unless it was the prelude to an attack. None of them looked over to the stage, nor appeared even to notice its existence.

McFadden said, 'Harriet, you had best crouch down on the floor.' Under other circumstances, she would have been thrilled to hear him use her Christian name in this way for the first time, but as things stood, Harriet was feeling almost too scared to give the matter much thought. She asked McFadden, 'Do you really think that there is any danger?'

'I think so, yes,' he replied. At almost precisely that moment, there was the crack of a rifle shot and the glass in one of the doors shattered, showering them with fragments and splinters.

'Get down, right now,' McFadden told her in a commanding voice, 'and mind where you put your hands; there is broken glass everywhere.'

Because she spent the whole of the time that the shooting was going on crouched on the floor, Harriet didn't really know what was happening. All she could hear were a variety of bangs, some coming from inside the stage and others from without. That and the stink of gunpowder were the only vivid memories that she retained of this incident in later life. Apart, that is, from the fact that when the shooting died down and she raised her head cautiously, the first thing she saw was the old gentleman lying back in his seat with a peaceful expression upon his face. She thought at first that he must have fallen asleep during the fighting, which struck her as odd, but then she saw a dark stain on his jacket and a glimpse of crimson splashed on his shirt-front. His eyes were open, but he was stone dead.

'That was too hot and strong for them,' said McFadden, turning from the window. He looked as though he were having the time of his life. His cheeks were glowing and his eyes were sparkling. What to her had been the most terrifying few minutes of her entire life was to him just a bit of sport. When he saw that the old man had not made it, he at least had the decency to look a little sobered.

The other man in the coach was reloading his pistol with practised movements, his eyes scanning the landscape outside as he did so. 'You have been involved in this sort of thing before, I think?' said McFadden, to which the man replied, 'Yes.'

'It's all right to get up now,' McFadden said to Harriet, reaching down to assist her. Lying on the floor had done nothing for Harriet's travel sickness and she was suddenly overcome with nausea.

He must have seen it in her face, because he said gently, 'If you are going to vomit, then lean from the window.' She did so and almost immediately threw up copiously.

As she was sick, Harriet began to shed tears of sheer mortification at the idea of anybody, particularly a man, seeing her in such a state. Even when her stomach was utterly empty, she still kept leaning out of the window, wondering how in the world she would ever be able to look Patrick McFadden in the eye again. She felt an arm around her shoulders and McFadden said quietly, 'Come and sit down now. You've had a shock.' She allowed herself to be guided back into the seat and then, just when she felt that her embarrassment could not become any worse, she began weeping like a child.

From all that she had seen of Patrick McFadden, Harriet would have bet good money that he was not a man with much patience for women who carried on in this way, having fits of the vapours. To her surprise, though, he was all kindness and consideration.

'It's all right,' said McFadden, 'it's all over now.' He put his arm around her shoulders and offered her his handkerchief and before she knew it, she was sobbing loudly and uncontrollably. The dark-skinned man sat staring from the window.

'I'm guessing that you have not seen anybody die like that in front of you,' said Patrick McFadden. 'It is fine to be upset about it. You would be unnatural were it not to shake you up. It is nothing to be ashamed of.'

'He was such a pleasant old gentleman,' said Harriet.

'He was a game one and no mistake,' said McFadden admiringly. 'He could not have been a day under sixty-five and yet he was as cool as they come.' He addressed the other passenger directly, 'What about you, sir, are you all right?'

'Yes,' said the man.

'Not what you expected on this

journey, I'll be bound?'

'No.'

'Why did they shoot at us?' asked Harriet.

'I couldn't say,' said McFadden. 'There is a lot of devilment afoot and that was all of a piece with it. They were Mescaleros. Very closely allied to the Apaches, but somewhat different. I heard that some of them had left the reservation, and thought that they too might be making for the Indian Territories. Apparently not.'

'Do you think . . . ' asked Harriet and left the question hanging in the air.

'Do I think that there will be any more shooting? I honestly couldn't say, Harriet. You will, I suppose, recollect that I was dead set against your coming on this journey?' She nodded penitently, but inwardly, despite all the shock and upset, she was exulting in the fact that they seemed now to be on first-name terms.

★　★　★

Dexter and Gonsalez rode into Phoenix just an hour before the stage got in. The two men were dead beat, but felt that before they could rest, they needed to track the movements of Gabriel Thorndike's niece and her friend. Both felt that it was her friend who was liable to queer the pitch for them. Leon Gonsalez and Alfred Dexter had both acquired over the years an infallible knack for sensing who could safely be preyed upon and who was better let alone. The hard-looking young man with Thorndike's niece definitely fell into the category of those best left alone. For all his smart appearance, both men could tell by instinct that dealing with this fellow was likely to prove a hard row to hoe.

* * *

As the stage entered Phoenix, Harriet Thorndike peered out of the window, drinking in the novelty of the new town. She had recovered very well from the

170

shock of the gunfight and even a night spent sleeping upright in the shaking coach had not been able to dent her spirits. She had at first wondered how on earth she would be able to sleep with a dead man sitting opposite her, but young people are adaptable and once her eyes were closed she soon forgot about the old gentleman and dozed off. When she woke, she found that her head was resting on Patrick McFadden's shoulder, but this did not seem to trouble him. She had started to apologise, but he said, 'If my shoulder is of any use to you, then please do not hesitate to take full advantage of it.' This sent her off into a fit of the giggles. She felt that this was not altogether fitting, with a corpse sitting opposite, and when she saw the other passenger looking at her oddly, she said, 'I'm sorry, I did not mean to cause offence.'

He answered, 'No.'

Although at home in Boston Harriet had a reputation for being a tough and forthright young woman, someone who had, as her mother remarked sadly, driven off several very eligible suitors with her bluntness, she was starting to enjoy allowing Patrick McFadden to organize things on her behalf. Perhaps it was that most of the young men she associated with in Boston were really just boys, something which nobody could have said about McFadden. Whether or no, she allowed him to arrange a hotel and organise the transport of their luggage there.

'Do you feel up to breakfast?' asked Patrick.

Harriet had called him by his first name the previous night and the world did not come to an end. She dared not think what her mother would have said about all this.

'I'm starving,' said Harriet. 'How are we to get up that mountain and when are we leaving?'

'That remains to be seen. Not today, at any rate. We will need to have a serious talk about this, Harriet. This is not a game now.'

'I know.'

The hotel was a comfortable one and after she had changed and washed, Harriet met Patrick in the dining room. The late breakfast or early dinner was substantial, consisting of eggs, bacon, kidneys and toast, all washed down with pots of coffee. Neither Harriet not Patrick McFadden were inclined to talk while eating. They were both famished and gave their full attention to the food for half an hour or so.

When they had finished eating, McFadden said, 'I need to visit the telegraph office before we make any sort of plans. There are sure to be messages for me and I must report back to my bosses.'

'Bosses?' said Harriet. 'Why, how many do you have?'

The man gave a wry smile. 'That is by way of being an uncertain point,' was all that he would say. He then went on, 'If you are really determined that you will not just put the whole matter into my hands, then I suppose

173

that we could hire ponies and head out to Superstition Mountain tomorrow morning. I tell you now, though, it will not be in the nature of a picnic, nor anything like. I had hopes that the episode on the stage here would have quenched your thirst for adventure.'

Harriet said nothing. How could she tell him that if it was a desire for excitement and the chance to travel which had first motivated her, it was now the desperate wish to remain in his company? This was not a thing that one could just announce to a man's face, or if it was, Harriet Thorndike, for all her modern ways, was not the girl to do it.

Patrick McFadden watched her face, but could make nothing of the mixed and changing emotions which he saw passing across it. For his own part, he too thought that the trip up to the mountain, dangerous though it would surely prove at this troubled time, would be more worthwhile with the girl's company than without it. He said, 'You won't reconsider?'

Harriet shook her head, not trusting herself to speak, lest the trembling in her voice betrayed her true feelings.

'Well then, I am going now to the telegraph office and will meet you back here in an hour or so. Does that suit?'

'I guess.'

Lingering outside, Gonsalez and Dexter were rewarded with the sight of Patrick McFadden striding from the Hotel Excelsior and heading downtown.

Gonsalez said, 'They are settled there now. They will not be going anywhere again this day, least of all out to the mountains. The talk at the depot was all about their coach being attacked by Indians. The girl will need a time to recover from the experience. I think that you and I can take the chance to rest ourselves, my friend.'

★   ★   ★

There were, as he had expected, a bunch of messages waiting for McFadden at the office. All were from

175

Washington and all were encoded. He took them back to the hotel to decipher.

In her room, Harriet was unpacking her trunk and withdrawing an item of clothing that she had possessed for several months, but never quite summoned up the courage to wear in public. It was a bloomer suit; exceedingly stylish, but quite outrageous. If it would have been outrageous on the streets of Boston, she could only imagine the stir it would create in a little town out west like this. Still, it seemed to her the most practical costume if she and Patrick were really to go horseback riding in the morning. She had never been riding in her life and hoped that it would prove as easy as it looked.

Harriet also took her uncle's gun from the trunk and, after finding the catch by trial and error, managed to open the cylinder and load the thing. She popped the weapon into her reticule. If she became embroiled in another affair of the type that had developed during the journey from Fenton's Creek, well then, this time she meant to be prepared!

In his own room at the Excelsior, just a few yards along the corridor from Harriet's, Patrick McFadden was sitting thoughtfully, having decoded the last of the messages that he had received. In the main, they were encouraging. The army had succeeded in halting some of the exodus from the reservations and heading off a number of the groups making for the Indian Territories. This, combined with an informal assurance to the leaders of the Five Civilized Tribes in the Territories that an application for statehood would be favourably received in a year's time, might just be enough to keep the lid on things for the time being. Geronimo and his band of Chiricahua were, as always, an unknown quantity and there was no telling what he was planning. It was the last of the telegrams at which he had looked that was perturbing McFadden.

The Commissioner for Indian Affairs himself specifically directed his Special Assistant, one Patrick McFadden, to give every aid to a survey team that was heading west. This team was working under the direct orders of the US Treasury and their intention was to meet up with McFadden so that he could hand over all the information in his possession, whatever it might be, that touched upon gold deposits in the region of Superstition Mountain. One did not need to be all that astute to see that Uncle Sam was minded to seize the biggest reef of gold that had ever been heard of for his own use.

Well, it wouldn't do; that was all. He, Patrick McFadden, had pledged his word of honour on this matter and he was not about to be made a liar by those thieving rascals. That gold would be used solely for the benefit of the Indians or it would not be used at all and there was an end of it.

There was a tap at Harriet's door. She hastily thrust the bloomer suit back into her trunk as she called, 'I'm coming, wait a moment please.'

Patrick McFadden was standing there when she opened the door and he did not look too happy. 'Harriet,' he said, 'will you come for a walk now, so that we might look into hiring ponies for a day or two?'

'Why yes,' she said, 'I shall be right down. I'll meet you in the lobby in five minutes.' She paused and then said, 'Is anything the matter?'

'It might be so,' replied Patrick. 'I'll see you downstairs.'

* * *

Over in a much cheaper establishment than the Excelsior, Leon Gonsalez was snoring noisily. Dexter was lying on his own bed, watching the Mexican's chest rise and fall and wondering when the time would be ripe to rid himself of his partner's company. If Alfred Dexter was not able to extract a bit of information from a young woman, then he wasn't the man he had always thought himself to be. As for the other, her companion or lover or whatever the hell he was, that would take a little more cunning. He was a sharp one by the look of him and he had already shown himself ready and willing to use force at the drop of a hat. The memory of fleeing from the Thorndike place like a frightened cur, with that bastard shooting at him, still stung somewhat. But that was nothing to the purpose, because Alfred Dexter made not the least doubt that he would be able to settle up that debt before long as well.

★ ★ ★

The two young people walked down the street together to the stables on the edge of town where McFadden had heard that ponies might be hired. As they walked, he spoke seriously to Harriet.

'I don't know how much you trust me, Harriet,' he said. 'You might think that all this stuff I have said about your uncle is just nonsense and that I am trying to trick you into revealing what you know.'

'Well,' said she, 'I did wonder. But now I know that my uncle really did like you. He trusted you as well.'

Patrick McFadden stopped dead and asked, 'How the deuce can you possibly know that? You didn't know before and now you have received assurances from beyond the grave? What is this, communing with the spirits or some such?'

The girl laughed. 'Hardly that. No, he left a book in which he wrote down a lot of stuff about his private dealings. He mentioned you.'

'All right, time for plain speaking. Do you have some sort of plan or map or list of directions, such as would make it possible for you to find this goldfield up on the mountain?'

'Yes, I do. But it would need your bit

of metal and a compass to enable anybody to follow the trail.'

Patrick looked at her, wondering not for the first time to what extent he should trust her. True, he was beginning to have personal feelings for her; that was quite another matter from letting her in on government business. He made a sudden decision. 'Look, Harriet. Say, you don't mind my using your name so, I hope?'

'No,' she replied boldly, 'I like it . . . Patrick.'

'Here is the case as it stands. The government will offer the Indian Territories the chance to become a fully fledged state of the union. They aim to do this in a year or so, at the same time that Oklahoma applies for statehood. This is conditional upon all the current upheaval ending. There seems to have been an agreement reached about this. There are, though, two flies in the ointment.'

Harriet listened without interrupting. 'The first of these little difficulties concerns Geronimo and his men. The rumour is that as a token of Apache good faith, he is leading representatives of other tribes up to Superstition Mountain. You might know that the location of that gold has always been a closely guarded, even sacred, secret of the Apache in general and the Chiricahua in particular?'

'My uncle wrote something of this,' said Harriet slowly, 'although I mind that he was given permission to go up there and even make a note of the route.'

'Do you know why they let him keep going back over the years?'

'Yes. He was selling the gold on behalf of the Indians and then handing the money over to them.'

'Which,' remarked McFadden, 'was suspected and makes everything a lot clearer.'

'I don't understand, though. Why should it matter if Geronimo tells the other Indian tribes where the gold is? Surely you, too, want the gold to be used for their benefit or to help this new state of theirs?'

'The problem is that I don't think that anybody except the government will be getting a share of this.' He told her about the survey team travelling to Phoenix and of his instructions to cooperate with them by handing over any information he had.

★ ★ ★

That evening, after they had had a good long sleep, Gonsalez and Dexter went out to see the town a little. They were on foot, judging it the smart move to let their horses rest properly after the hundred-mile dash from Fenton's Creek.

'We will need to stick to those two like cockleburs,' said Dexter thoughtfully. 'I am of the opinion that we should get up right early tomorrow and set a watch upon that Excelsior place. I mind that they might be setting out at first light or something.'

'Since teaming up with me, your wits have sharpened,' said Gonsalez, 'but still, you are right.'

'What do you reckon to this Apache business? Do you think it likely to interfere with our own plans?'

'Pah,' said Gonsalez, irritably, 'do not talk to me of Apaches. No, I don't see it. The army will be on Geronimo's tail and like as not chase him into Mexico. With good fortune, it will only be the four of us up on that mountain in a day, two at the most.'

'I am of the opinion,' said Dexter, 'that this will take careful handling. There is no manner of use just shooting that fellow first and trusting that the girl knows the whole story.'

'No, you are in the right about that. We must talk over a plan. We needs must question the pair of them. I guess that one knows one thing and the other something else. Why otherwise would he burden himself with the woman?'

'Maybe he's in love with her?' suggested Dexter, which provoked a snort of derision from the other.

The two men found Phoenix to be an agreeable enough place to spend an evening. When trouble erupted, it was not, as might have been expected, due to Gonsalez' temper, but was to be laid squarely at the door of Alfred Dexter.

9

Early on in the evening, Gonsalez had said, 'What would you say to the company of a woman?'

'Meaning what?' asked Dexter. 'Visiting a Hurdy or similar?'

'Why no,' said the Mexican, 'I had in mind a sporting house.'

'From what I recall, you lost all your money at cards the other night. You are asking me to pay for a prostitute to pleasure you?'

'Ach, we shall soon be rich. You begrudge me a few dollars now? Who was it put you onto this whole business? If not for me, you would be out on the road this night, waiting for some lone traveller who you could rob of a dollar or two.'

Dexter turned the proposition over in his mind for a spell, before finally conceding the point. 'I will allow that there is some merit in what you say. Since I have some money and you have none, then I do not see why the two of us should not go to a cathouse this night.'

Gonsalez, who seemed to have a sixth sense for anything at all disreputable or dishonest, had already located a brothel which was combined with a saloon. The girls mingled with the men drinking in the barroom and then, if an agreement was reached, took them upstairs. One might have thought that nothing could go wrong with such a simple arrangement, but men such as Alfred Dexter and Leon Gonsalez were more than able to create disorder from nothing at all, at the least provocation.

Once the two men were comfortably ensconced in the saloon and had drinks in their hands, they sat down at a table. It did not take too long before a couple of girls came over and began to be friendly towards them. This was all well and good; just precisely what they had come to the place for, in fact. Things went wrong when one of the girls draped herself over Dexter's lap and began nibbling his ear, into which organ she poured various lewd suggestions for the fun that they might be able to have upstairs. This was all most pleasant and agreeable and was of course just why Dexter had gone along with the idea of visiting a brothel.

Things went sour at the point when Alfred Dexter chanced to notice that the girl on his lap not only had her tongue practically in his ear, but had also managed to insinuate her slender hand into his pocket, from which she was attempting to remove as many bills as she was able. When he became aware of this new and unwelcome development, Dexter thrust the girl from him, almost sending her sprawling to the floor. 'Why, you little bitch!' he cried and then landed a solid punch in her mouth, which loosened a couple of her teeth. After this, events moved rapidly.

One of the fellows employed to deal with unruly customers approached

Dexter, presumably with a view to throwing him out. Before he reached Dexter, though, Gonsalez stuck out his foot and sent the fellow flying to the floor. As he fell, Dexter himself swung his foot into the man's ribs, cracking one. Then, all thoughts of lovemaking forsaken, Gonsalez and Dexter fought their way out of the bar. This was the signal for general mayhem, with other fights beginning apparently for no reason in different parts of the room.

'Well, that went well,' said Dexter, once the two of them were clear of the street in which the saloon was situated. 'We got all that we could have desired, apart, that is, from a woman.'

'You tell me that I am too quick to anger,' said the Mexican. 'I would say that the boot is all on the other foot as regards that. Why did you hit the girl so hard?'

'She was trying to pick my pocket. What else do you expect me to do?'

While these wild capers were occurring in one of the less salubrious parts of Phoenix, Patrick McFadden and Harriet Thorndike were having dinner together at the Hotel Excelsior. The plan was that they would have an early night and start out at first light for the Superstitions, which was what folk in Phoenix called the range of low mountains in which the lost mine lay.

'You have, I suppose,' said McFadden, 'some suitable clothes for riding?'

'Why yes,' said Harriet, a little defiantly, 'I think that I have the very thing.'

'You brought a riding habit in your trunk, just on the off chance that you would be getting on a horse?' asked McFadden curiously.

'Not exactly. It does not signify; I have an outfit which will meet the case perfectly.'

Both Patrick McFadden and Harriet Thorndike found the meal exceedingly pleasant. They began to behave like a normal couple; a young man and woman enjoying each other's company. At about ten, they parted. After the gruelling ride in the stagecoach, both felt in need of a good night's sleep. McFadden saw Harriet to her room and then, greatly daring and wondering what the response would be, he kissed her cheek. She gripped his arm for a second, returned a kiss to his cheek and then hurried into her room. So confused was she that she almost slammed the door behind her.

Before getting undressed and going to bed, Harriet took her uncle's book and read the final entry, which, judging by the content, could not have been made long before his death.

From all that I have been able to see, there is enough gold on Superstition Mountain to finance a small country. There is precious little in the Indian Territories to pay for all the things that a new nation would be needing. Trust my fellow countrymen to ensure that they only chose for the Indians the most barren and least promising land that could be found. On most of the reservations, there is barely enough to allow those living there to grub out their lives as subsistence farmers. The gold will change all that.

I am not myself a geologist, but have spoken to some who are learned in that field. From my descriptions, they tell me that the seam which surfaces at Superstition Mountain probably runs deep underground. The fragments of gold that have been worn away by the wind and sand are enough to provide incalculable wealth. Lord knows how much more lies hidden. There are trusty men who will be prepared to stake legal claim to this gold. White men, but men who are honest and will act as 'fronts' for the Indians.

In a month, Goyahkla will lead his men out of the San Carlos reservation and head for the Superstitions. There, they will take enough gold to pay for the initial expenses involved in the declaration of independence. Now I must state the thing plainly. I have an *idea that the government in Washington will not tolerate this venture. Imagine what the people of Texas or Georgia would make of it, if a part of the United States were to be allowed to secede like this! I have told Goyahkla that most likely the leaders of the Five Civilized Tribes will be offered a compromise; that is to say, statehood. I have also told him that he and they would be wise to accept such a proposition.*

I am not a young man, as God knows. I never thought that I would live long enough to see the dawning of this day, but with a little good fortune, I shall. I have given some information to McFadden from the Bureau. I might not trust that rascal of a boss of his, but Patrick McFadden is an upright and trustworthy fellow. I am sure that he will, when it comes down to it, do what is right.

By the time Harriet came to the end of her uncle's book, the tears were sliding down her cheeks. All his life, her Uncle

Gabriel had tried to do what was right and live an honest life. That some wretch had snuffed out that worthy life in a moment, filled the girl with fury. She prayed that one day the opportunity would present itself for her to take revenge upon the person who had killed her beloved uncle.

She put the book carefully to one side, put on her nightgown and got into bed. For all that she was still feeling upset about her uncle's death and also more than a little scared about what the next day would bring, Harriet Thorndike was also tremendously excited. Her last thoughts before falling asleep were of neither her uncle's murder nor the fabulous treasure which evidently lay waiting up on the nearby mountain. They were of a good-looking young man who worked for the government; a man whom her uncle had trusted implicitly. With this comforting reflection, the tired girl let slumber come to carry her away.

★　★　★

The two men who were hoping to torture and perhaps also rape Harriet Thorndike the following day were not yet asleep. Instead, they were bickering about the events of that evening. 'And after this,' said Gonsalez, 'still we did not have a woman.'

'I can't help that,' said Dexter, 'I was willing to pay. I will not be robbed, though, by man, woman or child.'

'We must make the most of that girl tomorrow then,' said the Mexican, with a determined note in his voice. 'It would be a sin to waste the chance. First the information, then we kill the man and ravish the woman. You agree?'

'You surely have a pretty way of putting things you know, Gonsalez,' said the other. 'I never heard the like. I'll warrant there never was such a man for plain speaking. But yes, as long as we take her turn and turn about, I am agreeable to that.'

'But that other, though, him we kill as soon as we find out all that he knows. Is that agreed?'

'It's nothing to me. I don't want to take advantage of him the way I would that girl. Sure, we kill him as soon as may be.' With which agreement, the two of them called it a day and settled down to rest for the night.

* * *

The next morning at breakfast, Patrick McFadden received one of the greatest shocks of his life when Harriet appeared at the table sporting her lime-green bloomer suit.

'What on earth are you wearing?' he asked, in unfeigned astonishment.

'It's a bloomer suit,' the girl told him, a little defensively. 'They are all the rage in New York.'

'Well I have spent a good deal of time in New York in recent months and I can assure you that I never saw anything of the sort. Where the devil did you get it?'

'I sent off for it through the mail,' answered Harriet in crestfallen tone, 'I thought it looked real stylish.'

'I suppose,' said McFadden, trying his best not to smile, 'that it might be just the thing for riding. Speaking in general, though, I think I prefer skirts. Are you really proposing to appear on the streets in that article?'

'Well I prefer a skirt too, to tell you the truth. It's just that I heard that all the smart people are wearing bloomers this year and I wanted to be in the fashion. I think it looks pretty awful really. What do you think?'

'I think it looks pretty awful as well, but I suppose that it will do well enough for riding.'

The two of them gulped down a hasty meal and collected the provisions that they had requested the kitchen staff to prepare for them the previous day. McFadden had told everybody that he was taking the young lady up into the hills for a picnic. He had contrived to make it sound as though this was a romantic assignation of some sort. The last thing needed was for anybody to get it into their heads that there was to be any prospecting or aught of that sort.

The Phoenix Examiner, the local newspaper, was full of news about Geronimo and his exploits. McFadden read through the whole account carefully, but it added nothing to what he already knew. He guessed that the fact was that nobody actually knew where Geronimo was or what he was up to.

As they walked along the street to the livery stable, McFadden said to Harriet, 'I suppose that you have the directions with you? You have not forgotten them or anything?'

She looked offended. 'Of course I have not forgotten them. They are right here in my reticule.'

'Your what? That is not a word with which I am familiar.'

'My reticule. This bag, see?'

'Give me some idea of what they say.'

'It all seems pretty straightforward, except where there are instructions such as 'walk cat for half a mile'. I imagine that that refers to some compass direction. Never mind my forgetting things, I suppose you have remembered to bring your compass?'

'Don't you fret about that,' said McFadden, 'I have everything which is needful. Where are we supposed to start from?'

'According to what I have seen, there is a tall, high spike of rock to the far west of the mountain. Once we find that, then everything else should be fairly easy. Are you aiming to stake a claim to this gold field, once we find it?'

Patrick McFadden did not reply. It was not that he was being evasive; he honestly did not know what he would do, if and when they reached the area which contained the gold.

By the time they got to the stable from which they were hiring the ponies, Phoenix was coming to life around them. The shutters were being thrown back on shop fronts, people were heading to work and the traffic in the streets was beginning to pick up. Among the carts and individual riders were two unremarkable figures whose horses were plodding along at the slowest of walks. Every so often, these two would rein in their horses and engage in conversation. It was not always easy for men on horseback to tail pedestrians without making it too obvious. Gonsalez and Dexter were hoping to see the man and girl mount up and head out. They would then race on ahead and prepare an ambush somewhere up on the mountain and out of sight of the town.

There were two sturdy little ponies waiting for Harriet and McFadden. The owner of the livery stable had assured them that if they were planning on trekking up into the Superstitions, then these critters would be a good deal more suited for the job than any thoroughbred. One of the ponies was a piebald and the other a grey. Harriet chose the piebald and before mounting, made friends with him by the simple expedient of handing him a lump of sugar which she had purloined from the breakfast table that morning.

As he watched Harriet's efforts to get on to the pony, the man who was leasing them the animals observed, 'Ain't ridden before, is that the strength of it?'

'I can manage,' said Harriet coldly. Eventually, she managed to hoist herself on to the piebald's back. Her reticule she hung around her neck. The weight of the pistol in it made the pressure from the strap uncomfortable, but there was no other choice. Since she also had the set of instructions in Pig Latin that would, she hoped, enable them to reach the gold, it was vital that the bag did not fall off during the journey.

'Will I expect you back today?' asked the livery stable owner.

'I surely hope so!' replied McFadden.

Once they were clear of the stable, which was on the very edge of town, McFadden said to Harriet, 'Let's see this famous treasure map of yours. I don't want you leading me a merry dance up on that mountain, just because you can't tell your north from your south.'

Without saying a word, Harriet opened her reticule and took out the directions, handing them to McFadden. He looked at them in surprise, before laughing. 'Old Mr Thorndike was not much of an expert on codes, if this was the best he could come up with. Pig Latin! I have not seen this since I was at school.'

'I'll thank you just to hand that right back, Patrick,' said the girl. 'I will tell you when we need to turn in any direction. For now, all we have to do is head straight for that rocky spire which we can see even from here. My uncle called it the needle.'

10

It took McFadden and Harriet the best part of the morning to reach the foothills leading up to Superstition Mountain. Before they started up into the hills, they stopped for a while to rest. Patrick McFadden was an experienced rider, but Harriet was beginning to feel very achy and uncomfortable. They had progressed mainly at a trot but, with Patrick's help and encouragement, interspersed with several bouts of cantering.

'Let's have that map of yours out, Harriet,' said McFadden. The girl opened her bag and, because it was tilted at an awkward angle, out fell her uncle's pistol. 'God almighty, why are you carrying that cannon?'

'After the trouble with Indians on the way here, I thought that it would do no harm at all to be prepared.'

'Have you ever fired a gun?' enquired Patrick pertinently.

'You just tend to your own affairs, Patrick McFadden, and leave me to tend to mine. I know that you must pull the trigger and I guess that is about enough.'

'Just do me the favour,' said McFadden, 'of making sure that I am not in the vicinity when first you essay a shot. I am minded that your friends will be in as much danger as your foes.'

Harriet pulled a face at him and then turned away, reddening at the thought of how free she was becoming with a grown man who was essentially a stranger. All this business was like one of those romances of which she had heard when folk went on vacation. She had not the remotest idea how it would all translate into real life, when she went back to Boston and Patrick returned to Washington.

'I can still see that spire that your uncle called the 'needle',' said Patrick. 'What must we be doing next? There seems to me to be but one route up into the hills from here. I calculate that we are just precisely due west of the 'needle'. What are we to do?'

Harriet took out the map and smoothed it out on the ground in front of them. 'For the Lord's sake make sure that that piece of paper does not blow away,' said Patrick urgently. 'Here, let me weight it down with stones. There, that's safe enough.'

'According to this,' said the girl, 'we must approach the needle from this direction and then, when we reach the base of it, turn 'cat' for half a mile, until we reach a little gully heading 'sun'. You had best work those directions out for yourself.'

McFadden reached into the pack which he carried over his shoulder and withdrew the brass disc and a sturdy army compass. He inserted the compass into the circular hole at the centre of the piece of metal and aligned the needle of the compass to the letter 'N' on the disc. 'From all that I am able to apprehend,' he said, 'that means that we keep on and face the needle from the west. Then we travel south-east for half a mile, until we reach a gully heading north.'

'Well,' said Harriet, 'why don't we get on then?'

'As far as I was able to collect from your uncle, the mountains here are a regular labyrinth of gullies, caves, canyons and dead ends. We must be very sure what we are about.'

They remounted the ponies and guided them along the path which led up into the hills. At the top of the first ridge, McFadden looked back towards Phoenix and frowned at what he saw. Catching his expression, the girl said at once, 'What's wrong? It's not . . . not Indians, is it?'

'No, I don't think so. Did you notice two men trailing along behind us while we were making our way to the livery stable?'

'I don't believe so. Why?'

'I did, and now I think that those

same two men are coming along after us. They are perhaps two miles back and ambling along at the same pace as us.'

'Maybe they are just travellers.'

'I don't think so. When we stopped just now, so did they, and then did not begin to move again until we started up this trail. They are following us.'

The two of them sat there for a space, watching the men in the distance. Harriet noticed that after a minute or two, the riders stopped moving. Patrick was right; they were being trailed by men who wanted to keep a certain distance between them. 'What should we do?' she asked. It was a very strange thing, but back home in Boston, you might go a good long while before you heard Harriet Thorndike ask any man a question of this sort. Since she and Patrick McFadden had teamed up, though, it seemed the most natural thing in the world to ask for his advice and to act upon his decisions.

He said, 'I think that we should carry

on and just keep a wary eye on those others. It may be that they are simply curious about us. The story of the Lost Dutchman's Mine is pretty well known hereabouts. Maybe they just have it in mind that we know where the gold is to be found. I doubt many people will be coming up into these hills just at the minute, not with Geronimo on the warpath. It was bound to attract attention, for all that I represented it to be a lovers' tryst.'

'Did you indeed?' said Harriet wrathfully and then fell silent when Patrick McFadden turned to look at her. He said, 'Are you annoyed at the suggestion?'

'Come on, I thought you said that we should start moving again,' said Harriet, sounding more than a little flustered.

The land flattened out somewhat before they reached the needle of rock, which rose perhaps a hundred and fifty feet into the sky. This meant that Harriet and McFadden were, in effect, travelling across a little plateau. They could no longer see Phoenix; nor could they see more than a few hundred yards behind them.

*   *   *

As soon as their quarry disappeared over the brow of the hill up which they had been riding, Gonsalez and Dexter spurred on their horses and began to gallop towards the hills. Whatever they got up to now would not be in sight of anybody; they were pretty sure to have a deal of privacy once in the Superstitions, for whatever mischief they devised. Their plan was a fairly straightforward and uncomplicated one. It entailed riding up on the man and girl, claiming that they had news of Geronimo, who was heading into the Superstitions. They would make themselves out to be regular benefactors, who had caught sight of the travellers and at risk of their own safety, followed them to give warning of the peril into which they had unwittingly strayed. Then, when the moment was right, they would pull guns on the two and render them helpless. Once the man and woman had told all they knew, then they would kill the man, ravish the woman and probably end by killing her as well, before going after the Apache gold.

*　*　*

When they were nearly at the base of the pillar of rock which Gabriel Thorndike had called the 'needle', McFadden reined in his pony and said to Harriet, 'We will wait here awhiles, because unless I am very much mistaken, those two fellows following us will soon show up. We can see clear for about a mile and when once we see them, we shall trot on south-east, until we come to this gully which is mentioned in your uncle's instructions. If they stick with us that far, then they are definitely following us and we must act accordingly.'

'What does that mean?' asked Harriet.

'It means that I shall take whatever action I feel is necessary.'

Sure enough, after a short wait, the two riders came into view over the rise; there was not the slightest doubt now that they were coming after them. McFadden urged on his mount and he and the girl headed south-east.

* * *

'You reckon they are onto us?' asked Dexter, as the two riders ahead of them made off again, after having halted briefly.

'It could be the case,' said Gonsalez. 'Whatever chances, do not shoot the man. We must question him, for I believe that he is the one who knows most about this enterprise.'

'I don't see him starting to engage in any gunplay with that girl by his side,' remarked Dexter thoughtfully. 'He will parley with us, even if he suspects that we are up to no good. With two of us on to the one, we should be able to handle him.'

'Mind, though, the girl too may have knowledge that we need. If there is any action, then be sure not to kill her before we have spoken at length with her too.'

Dexter looked the other full in the face. 'I might perhaps be a little hasty with my fists, Gonsalez, but by my reckoning, you are the one who is too quick off the mark when it comes to killing. Set a watch upon your own actions. I ain't a-going to kill anybody yet awhiles.'

★　★　★

The gap between the two pairs of riders was slowly closing and it was hard for anybody to pretend any longer that a pursuit was not in progress. McFadden said, 'Do you think that you could

213

canter for a goodish spell?'

'I think so, although my . . . that is to say a certain part of my body is sore.'

'Really, though, you have only yourself to blame there, getting involved in a game of this sort. Come, I see what could be that gully that we are looking for. At least, there is a small canyon which heads north.'

'How can you tell without looking at the compass?' asked Harriet.

'City girl! Because it is about midday and that little gully is just exactly opposite to where the sun is in the sky. The sun is due south and so that place must be to the north of this path.' The two of them rode on and when they reached the entrance to the gully, McFadden said, 'Hold up, now. Ride into the canyon there and I will see what yonder fellows want. No,' he said urgently, as Harriet showed signs of wanting to debate the point, 'there is no time to lose. It might be life and death, Harriet. Just do as I say, please.'

'Well then, be careful.' She did as he

bade her and rode a little way into the gully and then waited to see what would happen next.

Patrick McFadden turned to face the two riders who were approaching at a walk. He made no aggressive move, but reached casually and inconspicuously into his pack and made sure that the pistol there was ready to pull at the first hint of trouble.

The two men reined their horses in about thirty feet from McFadden and nodded to him in a friendly enough way. One of them, who had a Spanish look about him, said, 'Good day to you, pilgrim. You are going up into the mountains?'

'So it seems,' replied McFadden noncommittally.

'That is our intention also,' said the man. 'We too are travelling in that direction. What say you that we all fall in together? Seeing, that is, that our paths lie together? You might have heard that the Apaches have left San Carlos? It is safer to travel in a larger party, rather than just one or two together.'

While the swarthy-looking fellow was talking, his friend was gradually and, he hoped unobtrusively, moving away from him, so that it was going to be difficult to watch the pair of them at the same time. McFadden knew by now without a shadow of doubt that these characters meant him ill. Had it not been for the presence of a vulnerable girl nearby, he would probably have challenged them openly and then seen how far they were prepared to go. As it was, he tried to smooth matters over by letting them know that he was on to them. He said to the Spanish fellow, 'You had best tell your partner to set right where he is and not try to get round behind me. Do not for a moment think that I do not know what you boys are about.'

Dexter laughed. 'You know what we're about do you, you cow-son? You don't know shit!' He spurred his horse and rode swiftly behind McFadden, while Gonsalez drew down on him with his pistol. To McFadden's absolute horror, he heard Harriet's voice, saying, 'You drop that gun, now.'

Harriet Thorndike had been peeping round the corner of the rock face and seeing, as it appeared to her, that Patrick was in difficulties, had decided to take a hand in matters. She was holding her uncle's hefty great .45, which she could barely keep levelled, so heavy was the weapon. Dexter turned and saw. He laughed contemptuously. 'What you going to do with that thing, little lady?' he said, whereupon Harriet pulled the trigger.

The bullet did not hit Alfred Dexter, but it was a close enough miss to make him fearful for his life. He rode down upon Harriet Thorndike, before she thought about firing the thing again, and knocked the gun from her hand. Then he dismounted and grabbed hold of the girl, aiming to drag her down from her pony. Seeing this, McFadden cried out angrily, went for his own pistol and turned to confront Dexter. In doing so, he presented his back to Gonsalez who, not believing that he would have a better opportunity than this, rode forward, leaped from his horse and launched himself at McFadden, knocking him from the pony. He fell to the ground heavily, his head striking a rock. For a minute or two he was too dazed to be sure what was happening and when he came to, he found both himself and Harriet Thorndike in the most unenviable of positions; at the mercy of the two men who had followed them from Phoenix.

'Ah, you are now awake?' said Gonsalez pleasantly, when he saw Patrick McFadden open his eyes. 'You have a little sleep, yes, a siesta?'

McFadden realized that his hands had been expertly tied behind his back, with a length of rawhide from the feel of it. He could see that Harriet had been served in a similar way. He didn't have many good cards that he could see, but there was no harm in trying to bluff these characters. He cleared his throat and said in a commanding tone of voice, 'Untie me, you fools, or you will be in deeper trouble than you ever knew in your life.'

The two men said nothing. He continued, 'I am a federal officer and if you continue to interfere with the execution of my duty, then you render yourselves liable to the most severe penalties at law.'

Gonsalez stretched out his leg and delivered a painful kick to McFadden's ribs. 'I have killed federal officers in the past. I am happy to do so again. What do you say to that?'

'I say, if you want to kill me, then you must do as you see fit. At least let the girl go. She has no part in this.'

Dexter said, 'What was the two of you coming up into these here hills for, anyway?'

McFadden attempted a leer and a man-of-the-world air. 'Come on, I am sure you boys must have taken a pretty girl on a picnic before? There is no more to the case than that. Let her go, she knows nothing about anything.'

'Strange,' said Leon Gonsalez. 'Strange if she is not connected with this mountain that she should have a map in her bag of the area. Why would she be carrying such a thing? And it is not in English either. And what is this?' He held up the brass disc that went with the compass. McFadden said nothing.

Gonsalez stood up and then bent low over McFadden. He said, 'I have some experience in questioning people. When I have finished with them, they are generally sorry that they have not got more information to give me. During the war against the French, in my own country, I was a famous man for my way with prisoners.'

'Yes,' said McFadden in a conversational tone of voice, 'you look just the kind of low whore's son who would have a liking for such games. You are a coward at heart, though. Untie me and then we will see how you fare man to man.'

Dexter said, 'Are we going to set here jawing all day or are we going to find out what we wish to know?'

'You speak truly, my friend,' said Gonsalez. 'We have played enough.' He drew from his boot the same slender stiletto with which he had killed the man in Fenton's Creek saloon. He squatted by McFadden's head and laid the blade on his cheek. 'Now, I will ask you about this map first. What language is this?'

The most that he and Harriet could hope for was to stretch out this whole process and then there was the slenderest of chances that somebody would come by and they might be rescued. Not that McFadden really set much store by this possibility. Still, it was all that there was to hold on to.

'I will tell you what you wish to know, if you will let us go,' announced Harriet unexpectedly and to McFadden's utter horror. For his part, he had not the slightest doubt that once these rogues had the knowledge which would enable them to reach the gold, then they would just kill the two witnesses. The only real question was whether they would rape the girl before killing her. His instinct told him that they probably would. All that Harriet's interjection had done was speed up their deaths.

'Don't set any mind to what that young fool tells you,' said McFadden roughly, 'she knows nothing about this.'

'Maybe,' said Dexter.

Gonsalez was tiring of all this talk and decided that the quickest way to get the man to surrender his knowledge was just to hurt him. He therefore drew the blade of his knife down McFadden's cheek. As the blood began to flow, Harriet gave a shriek of horror.

'What do you say now?' asked Gonsalez, 'Will you still be the tough man? Or do you want me to take out one of your eyes, next time?'

McFadden said nothing. Something

about his manner told the Mexican that this was not going to bring about the desired end and so he turned to his partner. 'You know what,' he said to Dexter, 'I think that this would work a lot easier if I were to use my knife on the girl instead.' Harriet gave a whimper of fear as Gonsalez stood up and walked over to her.

'Stop!' said McFadden, 'I will tell you what you need to know. Let the girl alone.'

Both Dexter and Gonsalez were grinning broadly now. This was the sort of setup which they relished. In this, they were very much alike, despite the superficial differences; they enjoyed having people at their mercy and making them do as they were bid.

'All right,' said Gonsalez, 'where were you heading?'

'To the place where the Apache gold is to be found,' replied McFadden. 'That map is not in a foreign language, it is English, just altered a little.' He explained the principle of Pig Latin and watched as Dexter slowly translated the directions to the lost mine.

'What's this here,' asked Dexter, 'about walking cat or heading sun?'

McFadden set out for him the importance of the brass disc and compass. He could see the exultation in the eyes of the two men who had waylaid them. They had everything they wanted and there was no other obstacle standing in their way. The gold was as good as theirs already.

All the talking and excitement had served to make Gonsalez and Dexter wholly involved with affairs in their immediate proximity. Neither of them were paying much heed to any noises in the distance; they were too busy congratulating themselves on their success in breaking the resistance of the man they were questioning. Had they not been so filled with triumph, then they might, like McFadden, have heard the approach of a small party of riders, who were treading their way carefully along the track from the opposite direction in which the others had arrived at the mouth of the gully. It was not until this group were almost on top of them that either Gonsalez or Dexter became aware that anybody else was up on the mountain.

The thirty or so Indians advanced their horses at a walk, until they were surrounding the four figures clustered together. It was apparent that any attempt at fighting would end at once in disaster, because these men were armed to the teeth and did not have the look of people who would hesitate to use violence. They sat on their mounts, surveying the scene before them. The man who was evidently their leader, a hard-faced fellow of about sixty, asked in good English, 'What are you doing on this mountain?'

Patrick McFadden decided to stake all on one throw of the dice and said boldly, 'We came here to help the Chiricahua. These men hope to steal the gold and they attacked us.'

The Indian leader looked at McFadden's face, which bore the marks of Gonsalez' work. 'What do you know of the Chiricahua?' he asked.

'I was a friend of Gabriel Thorndike,' said McFadden. 'He asked me to see that the gold on this mountain was used only to help the Indians. Now, apart from these two, men from the government are also coming to steal it.'

'You are a friend of Gabriel Thorndike?' asked the Indian.

At this point, Harriet called out, 'I am his niece. He had a good friend in the Chiricahua called Goyahkla. He knew my uncle and knew that he wanted to help the Indians to have a land of their own.'

The old Indian to whom they had been addressing these remarks dismounted and then stood for a time looking at the four people, as though working out what the play was. Then he turned to Gonsalez and said in an expressionless voice, 'Did you tie up these two?'

'Sure, but you got it all wrong,' said Gonsalez. 'We are working for the government and these two are thieves. We are taking them back to town now. We don't know anything about gold.' There was a thin sheen of sweat on his face and it was not hard to see that he was terrified almost out of his wits. He knew what happened to Mexicans who fell into the hands of the Chiricahua.

11

The leader of the Indians gave a few curt words of command to two of his men and they jumped off their ponies and went over to Harriet and McFadden. They then drew knives and slashed through the rawhide thongs, freeing the man and woman. Harriet stood up and rubbed her wrists, grimacing at the pain as the circulation returned. McFadden also stood up slowly and eyed the party of riders, all of whom looked to his practised eye as though they were ready to fight a war. He had not the least idea how this was going to pan out. It was altogether possible that rather than being murdered by one set of villains, he and the girl would fall prey to another.

The old Indian said to Harriet, 'What do you think my name is?'

'I couldn't guess.'

'Long ago,' he said, 'when I was fighting the Mexicans, they were so scared of me and my men that they called for the aid of their gods.' He stared into the distance as he remembered his youth. 'One time, I charged some soldiers. They were all firing at me and I had only this knife.' He drew a large knife, more like a dagger than anything else, with a blade which must have been at least eight or nine inches long. 'I ran at them with this, shouting the war-cry of my clan.'

The old man's face creased in pleasure at the recollection of the mad exploits of his youth. 'They were religious men and called out to Saint Jerome, who was one of their gods. They kept crying out, 'Jerome, Jerome, protect us Jerome'. None of their bullets hit me and my men ran after me. They followed me anywhere.'

The Indian fell silent and Harriet asked, 'What happened, sir?'

He laughed, 'What happened? I killed some and my warriors killed the rest.

Except that two men ran away. They ran so fast that we laughed and let them escape. Ever since that day, I have been called after their god, after this Jerome.'

'Your name is Jerome?' asked the irrepressible Harriet. 'That is a strange name for an Indian.' McFadden groaned to himself and wished that the girl would just shut up. Things were bad enough as they stood, without her annoying the men who, from all that he was able to collect, now held them captive.

'Jerome?' said the old Indian. 'Yes, they called me something like Jerome. Only the name was twisted over the years. Now, they call me Geronimo.'

The three white men and the woman stood thunderstruck at the casual way that the man revealed his identity. This then was the terrifying character whose very name had become synonymous with murder and pillage. The Indian saw their reaction and chuckled. He said, 'But I was not born Geronimo. That was not the name that my mother gave to her baby. She named me Goyahkla. In the Chiricahua tongue, this means 'he who yawns'.'

Patrick McFadden shifted uneasily. 'This is all well and good, sir, but we are wondering what you are going to do with us now?'

'I am not going to do anything with you,' said Geronimo. 'You and Gabriel's brother's child are free to leave. These others, though, I shall take with me. I think this one is Mexican and I always have a score to settle with Mexicans.' He turned to Harriet and bowed. 'It is good to meet you. Your relative is a good friend of every tribe.'

Harriet said, 'Oh, but you don't know. He is dead.'

'I knew him for most of my life. It is a grief to me to hear this. He was a man to trust.'

McFadden said, 'May I talk to you alone, sir?' Like Harriet, he found himself automatically addressing this man as 'sir'. It was strange, because it was not a title that he would usually accord to any Indian. There was a majesty about this man, though, which marked him out; set him apart as a great leader of men.

'I have no secrets from these people,' said Geronimo. 'They are not just of my own tribe, but also there are men here of the Sioux, the Cherokee, the Choctaw. I will not conspire out of their hearing. This day, all Indians are as brothers and will soon be members of one nation.'

'Yes,' said McFadden, 'I know something of this. You mean Sequoyah.' There were murmurs of surprise from the other Indians at hearing the word spoken out loud by a white man. Presumably, thought McFadden, the very name is like a password; the indication that one belongs to the conspiracy. He said, 'I do not mean to say anything against anybody, whether Apache or Sioux. I only want to tell you about your old friend Gabriel Thorndike and his last words on the matter of this enterprise in which all you men are engaged.'

Geronimo said something to the other Indians and then turned to McFadden. He said, 'Do you see that hill?' He pointed to a rocky bluff which towered above the track on which they were standing. 'We shall climb up there and talk. I wish to remain in sight of all these men, though.'

'Just as you will, sir.'

It was a hard scramble up the bare rock to the top of the bluff. Patrick McFadden was agile and fit enough, but he found it a tough task. The Indian, though, seemed to take no more effort over the climb than if he had been strolling along the sidewalk in a town. At one point, McFadden slipped and nearly went tumbling fifty feet down to the rocky surface of the plateau where the others waited. Geronimo whirled round swiftly and grasped his arm to steady him. 'Thanks,' said the younger man.

'How old are you?' asked the Indian leader, as they neared the peak.

'Twenty-nine.'

This answer seemed both to satisfy and amuse Geronimo. 'I am more than twice your age. When I was young, I could run up this rock. You hear me? Run! Now, I am an old man and have to climb like a woman.'

'You are still a sight better at the job than me,' said Patrick McFadden breathlessly.

'Yes,' said the Indian dryly, 'I have seen that.'

By the time that they reached the top of the rock, McFadden was feeling exhausted, but the Indian walked about as though he had just jumped out of bed. After giving the younger man a minute to recover, he said to him, 'Well, what are these secrets that you would tell me?'

'That your plans for Sequoyah are known to everybody, even the government. That the leaders of the Five Tribes have now agreed to being a state in the union and not an independent country. Also, the government is now heading here to try and take all the gold on this mountain and keep it for themselves. The Indians will not benefit from it at all. I'm sorry, but your gamble is finished.'

Geronimo thought over for a few seconds what had been said and then replied, 'I have brought men from other tribes here this day to show them the way to the gold. This is an act of openness and trust. I am going to share with them a great secret of the Apaches.'

'You do that and the government will be certain-sure to steal that gold. If you want it to be used for Sequoyah, then the only hope is to leave here now and then return when the state is declared. It might be next year, at the same time that Oklahoma is admitted to the Union.'

'How do you know so much of this?'

'I work for the government. Gabriel Thorndike trusted me. Between us, me and that niece of his can find the way to that little valley of yours. I am prepared to destroy the information we possess, though, if it will keep the government from taking that gold. It belongs to your people.'

'What do you think that is, over there to the east?' asked Geronimo.

'Your eyes are probably sharper than mine. I would say that it is a cloud of dust about eight or ten miles hence. At a guess, I would say that it is a column of cavalry.'

'So I also thought. Well, you may be speaking the truth or you may not. I think that you have a truthful face and for that alone, I shall leave you alive.' The old man smiled at McFadden, as though this was a great joke. 'We must go down quickly. Do you need my help?'

'I reckon I can manage, thank you, sir.'

'I would like to see how you do this in thirty years.' Having said which, the old man began skipping and hopping down the rocks with the agility of a young goat. He reached the bottom ahead of Patrick McFadden by a good margin and by the time that young man was down, the Indians were ready to move off. The two men who had waylaid him and Harriet were mounted on their horses and seemingly being taken off as prisoners of the Indians.

'Unless the Bluecoats have changed their ways, then by nightfall this mountain will be crawling with soldiers,' said Geronimo to Harriet and McFadden. 'There would be no purpose in showing my brothers from the other tribes where the gold is to be found. It would be making a gift of it to the enemy.'

'Where will you go?' asked McFadden.

'Where do the Indians go? Who knows where we will go? Perhaps south, perhaps north, west or east. Goodbye.' The old Indian turned to Harriet. 'Farewell to you. Your father's brother was the best of men, red or white. You may be proud of him.'

The band of Indians rode off, back

along the way that they had come. Within a few minutes, there was silence and the two young people were alone on the rocky plateau. They did not speak for a bit and then Harriet said, 'So that was Goyahkla. He was a most polite old gentleman. I'm glad I met him.'

'That's nothing to the purpose,' said McFadden. 'We need to figure out what we are going to do next.'

'What do you mean?' said the girl, sounding disappointed. 'I thought we were going to find this famous gold?'

'Goyahkla was right. He said that by nightfall these mountains would be swarming with soldiers. There is a column of cavalry heading this way. I would not be at all surprised to learn that they are escorting a field survey team whose job it is to find and secure the gold. If that happens, the Indians won't get a look-in. Uncle Sam will take the lot.'

A week ago, Harriet would have been disposed to argue the point, just to show that she was not going to be pushed around by some man. Now, she just said, 'What do you think we ought to do?'

'I think we should destroy that map of yours and get rid of this piece of brass. I don't want to be found with it in my possession, it might compromise me.'

'But if we do that, how will we ever find the gold in the future?'

McFadden said nothing. Harriet said, 'You don't think that we should? We should just leave it to the Indians, whatever they want to do with it?'

'I think that we would do more harm than good by interfering further. I promised your uncle that I would do what I could to ensure that any profit from that gold went direct to the Bureau of Indian Affairs. I can't do that and so I think we should not have any further part in it.'

'It would have been kind of nice to see all that gold,' said Harriet wistfully. 'Still, I suppose you are right.'

McFadden handed the girl a box of lucifers and she struck one and put it to the corner of the map. It flared up at once and was soon reduced to ashes. There remained the brass disc. They found a deep fissure in the rock, only an inch or so wide but very deep. They dropped the piece of metal in and then mounted their ponies and set off back to Phoenix.

★   ★   ★

By the time that Patrick and Harriet got back to Fenton's Creek, they had reached what is known as an 'understanding'. Which is as much as to say that they had agreed that they wished to get married. There was some debate about how they would live. The Commissioner for Indian Affairs was livid with his special assistant when he was told that there existed no solid evidence at all to lead anybody to the Apache gold. The Commissioner had apparently staked his political future on being able to provide the government with a huge amount of gold and was now discredited. Patrick felt obliged to resign both from this position and also his post with the army. About this second official role, he was very vague with his future wife.

In the end, it was agreed that the couple would travel to Boston and see what chanced. Not only did Harriet's mother live in that city, but Patrick also had relatives there; one of whom was persuaded to give him a job.

The wedding of Captain Patrick Michael McFadden, formerly of the United States Army, and Harriet Thorndike took place on Saturday July 16th 1886.

Epilogue

Goyahkla and his tribe remained at large for another two months, but were never able to return to Superstition Mountain. Nor were they able to reach the Indian territories. Even after they surrendered to General Nelson A. Miles in September 1886, none of the Chiricahuas were able to travel to their sacred mountain. The entire tribe, including the women and children, were shipped to Florida and held as prisoners of war. Later they were transferred to Alabama and then Fort Still in Oklahoma. They were not finally released until 1913; almost thirty years after the surrender. This captivity could have been cut short at any time, had the location of the gold been revealed. Not one of the prisoners who knew anything of the matter ever spoke of it.

Even the promised state of Sequoyah

did not in the end materialise. Promises were made to the Indians that if they were just a little patient, all would work out for the best. Without the aid which the gold on Superstition Mountain could have bought them, they had little choice but to be patient. In 1887, an act was passed in Washington which reduced the territory of the Five Civilized Tribes and when, a year later, they tried to apply for statehood, their application was brusquely refused by Congress. When Oklahoma applied for statehood a few months after that, the application was accepted. The territory of the new state included all the former Indian Territories and spelled the final end of Indian hopes of a recognized nation or even a state in the union of their own.

The gold of Dutchman's Mine was never found and still lies in a little valley in the Superstition Mountains. There have been many expeditions to hunt for the lost Dutchman's Mine; none have been successful.

We do hope that you have enjoyed reading this large print book.

Did you know that all of our titles are available for purchase?

We publish a wide range of high quality large print books including:
Romances, Mysteries, Classics
General Fiction
Non Fiction and Westerns

Special interest titles available in large print are:
The Little Oxford Dictionary
Music Book, Song Book
Hymn Book, Service Book

Also available from us courtesy of Oxford University Press:
Young Readers' Dictionary
(large print edition)
Young Readers' Thesaurus
(large print edition)

For further information or a free brochure, please contact us at:
Ulverscroft Large Print Books Ltd.,
The Green, Bradgate Road, Anstey,
Leicester, LE7 7FU, England.
Tel: (00 44) **0116 236 4325**
Fax: (00 44) **0116 234 0205**

VALLEY OF THUNDER

Sam Clancy

Josh Ford is the best man the Marshal Service has ever had, so when the governor of Montana needs someone to look into the disappearance of wagon trains in the Bitterroots, Ford is the man he chooses. What Ford finds is a brutal autocrat who rules with terror unlike Ford has ever seen. Across the northwest, he must fight against a maniac and his small army — but when a final twist puts it all in jeopardy, he realizes that the badge he wears may be the difference between law and justice.

RELUCTANT TIN STAR

Dale Graham

When Marshal Troy Garrison is forced to leave the Colorado town of Aguilar under a cloud, he figures he's done with the law for good. Heading south into New Mexico, he becomes embroiled in a series of unsavoury incidents culminating in his rescue of a damsel in distress. An unscrupulous gang of rustlers is terrorizing the area, and Troy reluctantly pins on the tin star once again. But when the woman's brother becomes involved with the gang, he is forced to choose between romance and upholding the law . . .

DAYS OF DEATH

P. McCormac

Elwood Black wants complete control over the gold mining community of Thomaston. He surrounds himself with killers such as Clive Carter, outlaw and deadly gunman, and the Goliath-like pugilist, Sheriff Goran Ginsberg. He makes one fatal mistake — his man Carter kills Cyriac Halkias' brother. Heavily scarred from previous deadly encounters, Cyriac rides to Thomaston. Those responsible for his brother's death must pay. The body count mounts as the days of death descend on Thomaston. Cyriac will not stop until the account of his vengeance has been paid in full.

ARCHER'S LUCK

Ed Roberts

When drifter Lew Archer meets a priest while travelling along a lonely road in Texas, he thinks nothing of it. But this chance encounter sets in motion a train of events which sees Archer escorting a party of nuns through hostile territory to start a school on the Mexican border. With war and bloodshed around them, Lew Archer is the best man to help them make their way to safety, although why he should take the trouble to do so is a mystery to everybody — including Archer himself!

THE LAWLESS BREED

Ralph Hayes

After Wesley Sumner is released from prison, he and cellmate Corey Madison go in search of work as ranch hands. But their newfound freedom is short-lived when they are arrested for a crime they didn't commit. And when Corey dies after a savage beating from their captors, Sumner vows revenge. When he learns that the two deputies who beat Corey have lost their jobs and are now themselves on the run from the law, Sumner begins a long and dangerous journey, slowly but surely tracking down his friend's killers.